MW01118336

BETRAYED BY SILENCE

Katherine Shephard

"Our lives begin to end the day we become silent
about things that matter."
—*Martin Luther King, Jr.*

SEVEN LOCKS PRESS

Santa Ana, California

Seven Locks Press
P.O. Box 25689
Santa Ana, CA 92799
(800) 354-5348

Individual Sales. This book is available through most bookstores or can be ordered directly from Seven Locks Press at the address above.

Quantity Sales. Special discounts are available on quantity purchases by corporations, associations, and others. For details, contact the "Special Sales Department" at the publisher's address above.

Printed in the United States of America

Library of Congress Cataloging-in-Publication Data
is available from the publisher
ISBN 1-931643-35-0

Cover and Interior Design by Sparrow Advertising & Design

Make yourself familiar with the angels, and
behold them frequently in spirit;
for without being seen,
they are present with you.

This book is dedicated to:
My Guardian Angels

Acknowledgements

CONTEST WINNERS:

David Sadoway—who created the character of Senator Blane MacGowen.

Kelly Hain for the inspiration to donate a portion of the proceeds from the *Silence Series* to animal rescue. This "tail" really DOES have a happy ending!

To my editor, Regan Marie Brown, and friend, Randy Rawls, for their constant nudging, critiquing, knowledge, and wit. You have counseled me wisely.

Thanks to Sharon Young, the Queen of Commas, and Randy, the King of POV. Also, Heather and Jim, of Seven Locks Publishing, for keeping on schedule just like promised.

Linda Bingham—the 'Best Lil WebMaven in Texas.'

My card girls for balancing me; Bonnie Brown for making me look good despite those bad hair days; Berni and Jimmy for *always* being there; the families and staff of Saddleback Valley Christian School for their prayers, and Shelly Wilburn—for her friendship, which was the inspiration used to create the character of Shelly Parsons in her likeness.

To Michael B. Lynch for taking time out of his busy schedule to train me on everything I wanted (and didn't want) to know about polygraph examination. I knew I didn't do it!

Jon Sultzer, D.V.M., and Roberta, *Laguna Hills Animal Hospital*, for sharing their expert medical advice on all things "B.A.D."

Mr. Brad Whittman—Michigan's *Secretary of State's Office* for teaching me about Section 22, Article 5!

Ray Rawlings of *Dana Point Piano*. Now I know what a midi-rail is!

The Michigan Department of Corrections for their assistance.

Tom Reiser—research librarian—my minister of information. The character of Father Tom is dedicated to you!

My family, most especially **Bob**—for being the "sole parent" when I've been on the road and to **RJ** for encouraging his mom to "go for it!" and for always saying "that's so cool!"

To the *FABULOUS* folks of **Grand Ledge, Michigan,** for always welcoming me "home"—and for providing the factual backdrops and characters that live amongst the fiction of *The Silence Series*. Especially Kelsie Violet Hough Black for lending me her mom and dad for this book.

Most especially,
I look to the Heavens and thank my mom and dad for believing I could soar.
They never clipped my wings. I miss you both so much.

December, 1998

Chapter 1

My best friend, Victoria, thinks drama
is the ultimate art form.
That morning she outdid herself.

"Bob! Chrissy! Get the hell out of bed. Now!" Victoria's shrill voice was not the alarm clock I had set the night before. Come to think of it, I hadn't set an alarm clock. Peeking under the covers, I realized we were safe. For once we were wearing pajamas. Bob made a groaning noise and pulled a pillow over his head as I sat up and stared at our intruder.

"Vic, what are you doing here at six in the morning on a Tuesday, and what are you doing in our bedroom with a negligee hanging below your jacket?" Panic set in, as I started wondering how she got in the house—not to mention why she was hysterical.

"The Veep talks in his sleep and I think someone's dead, or is going to be."

"The Vice President? You're sleeping with the damn Vice President?" My palms began to sweat, my breath came out in doubletime, and thoughts of what trauma awaited us now began to bubble up to the surface of my consciousness.

"Good God, no! It's Blane MacGowan! He used to be a judge here in Michigan. But his dad died and he inherited a whiskey company with his older brother. He's now the vice president of GlenGowan. Gave up the judge gig. He's something else, too. Everyone calls him Veep. Well, except for me. I call him the Hot Scot. His kilts are almost floor length. You can imagine why."

Bob, with eyes half-opened, brushed his hands through his hair and spoke. "Shit. Blane killed someone and decided to unload on you when he was asleep?" A slight grin swept across his face and he poured on his smooth Texas drawl. "Missy, are you just paranoid, or have you gone into your hyper-theatrical mode?"

Drama should have been Vic's major. Instead, she went the poli-sci route at our alma mater, Michigan State. She thought a major in politics would hook her up with powerful men. Looks like she was right.

Victoria planted her hands on her bony hips. Her cat-like eyes seemed to be on fire—I could feel them burning holes through the sheets. "No, I am not paranoid! He talked about you!"

Bob sat up and stared at my best friend. He's used to her melodrama and musical bed routine. "Not good. Doesn't reflect well on you, Vic. A man thinking of me when you're snuggled up to him."

Vic and I have known each other our entire lives and are as close as Siamese twins. I've seen her freak out over a missed period, a lost friendship ring, and my mother's death when we were only five years old. None of it came close to this.

I reached up and pulled her down onto the bed, hoping a more comfortable spot would unruffle her feathers. "Calm down. Start from the beginning. Skip the theatrics and the personal details, please." Vic has a way with men and she seldom finds herself munching popcorn and watching reruns alone in bed.

"Well, Blane was tossing and turning. That meant the covers left me and ended up on his side. I had the ceiling fan on and—"

"Vic! Stop already." I hate mornings. Anything before eleven a.m. should be outlawed. Being awakened by anything loud should be a felony, and so far Vic's appearance ranked right up there on the Worst Crimes of the Century list. She was in our bedroom. She was upset. The sooner we heard her tell the story, the sooner I got back to sleep. "What did he say about Bob?"

"He said . . . okay, this is a quote. I got right up and wrote it down. He said, 'Larken. Larken jury. Okay I will. Minnie'—or maybe it was Benny or something, it was kind of mumbled at that point. Anyhow, he was tossing and turning and saying, 'Jail. A Pandora's box. Larken. Can't get her out. Run.' That's when I got the hell out of there. Took me less than thirty minutes to get my ass over here from Grand Rapids, too. Even with the snow."

Despite the early hour, she had my attention. "Bob, do you know a Minnie or a Benny that's in jail?" I felt my journalistic curiosity waking up. This was my man. My husband of two weeks, give or take a few days. "Think, Bob. There has to be someone out there. Someone with a grudge?"

My questions were cut off by the gorgeous voice I fell in love with. "Okay—everyone up. Let's go downstairs and figure this out. Babe, I know how your mind is thinking—and Vic's mind. Let's not go there."

As the three of us started for the stairs, I saw our pup sleeping at the foot of our bed. Her rumpled pink blanket surrounded her in a cozy cocoon, and her gentle snoring gave testament to why the unusual ruckus hadn't awakened her. Once asleep it takes a major act of God or the smell of food to awaken her. I stopped in my tracks and turned towards Vic. "Wait! How *did* you get in?"

"Through the front door. It was unlocked. Stupid, leaving your door like that." She cut her eyes towards the two of us. "The newlyweds rush to get upstairs last night?"

Remembering our haste to get upstairs the night before, we both blushed. Bob motioned for us to continue down the stairs. "Move it. Both of you."

Once in the kitchen I began the coffee-making ritual. Never begin the day without a fresh pot of Michigan Cherry Java, that's my motto. As the coffee brewed, I looked out the large picture windows outlined in Christmas lights. Winters in Grand Ledge are magical. I could see the frozen Looking Glass River through the white-blanketed branches of the oak trees. A fresh coating of snow covered the ground, indented here and there by the tracks of foraging deer.

As the aroma of fresh coffee started to fill the kitchen, I kept staring out the window and reflected again on how lucky Bob and I were to have this refuge in the woods. Small-town living gave us the sense of belonging and the solitude necessary for the life of a politician. With the governor's inauguration only a week away, Grand Ledge was the perfect place for us to be: out of the way. Yep, Grand Ledge suited us fine. Solitude, serenity, and people discreet enough not to pry into our business.

Suddenly I became aware of Victoria standing over me, glaring, with eyes reminiscent of Charles Manson. Being seven inches taller than me, she's always had the physical advantage of intimidation by stature. "Chrissy, you're not listening to me!" Her rampage continued. "You're off in another one of your stupid daydreams. That's what got us in this mess in the first place. You sitting around pining for Mr. Dreamboat here. You just had to go off and hook up with a married politician, then his wife dies, and *tada!* You get married and live happily ever after. Hasn't anyone bothered to tell you fairy tales are a bunch of crap?"

With that snide comment, Vic tossed her hair back and crossed her arms. Her black, straight hair hung to her chin on one side and was closely cropped on the other. Lopsided and totally Vic. When she was upset, the skin on the right side of her scalp turned red. It was now three shades beyond the radiance of the Texas granite Bob adored.

"Great way to start my morning. Appreciate it, Vic." I really, really hate mornings.

Bob broke off our sarcastic banter. "Okay, ladies, listen up. This is about a dream. A guy who talks in his sleep. This is not Watergate—it's a dream! Vic, thanks for the concern but believe me, I don't know anyone in jail. Well, not personally at least. I'll think about whom I might have alienated when I was a broadcaster, but nothing comes to mind right now. Trust me, okay?"

Victoria, looking incredulous, continued. "Kind sir, excuse me if I don't take you up on that offer." Vic's eyeball rolling was an art form. "You're a former politician. A former broadcaster. Definitely a man. Three strikes—you're dead."

That was it for me. "Vic, please. That's sick. Anyhow, it's three strikes, you're out."

Glaring back, she never missed a beat. "Out. Dead. Either way it's scary. Blane was not talking in his sleep—he was tossing, turning, sweating."

I could have sworn she was smiling when recounting the moment.

Bob nodded his head. "I remember Blane. He knows John, too. I think John helped with his election campaign when he ran for judge."

Just the mention of John Gaynor brought Bob to life. John was Bob's mentor—a well-heeled and influential man who seemed to know all the right people and had been the brains and wallet behind Bob's rise from broadcaster to politician, turning him from a name *on* the news to a name *in* the news. When Bob became lieutenant governor of Texas John covered his back, professionally and personally. A few months ago we discovered he was also Bob's biological father.

Bob's recognition of her latest paramour was all the fuel Vic needed to continue. "So, what do you make of it? Why the panic? And it's early, I know, but do you have any cookies? I crave sweets when I panic."

We heard what sounded like a herd of elephants bounding down the stairs and saw a flash of white fur skidding across the freshly waxed kitchen floor. How could one small puppy make so much noise running down a flight of carpeted stairs?

"Vic. You said the magic word. *Cookies.*" Bob and I both laughed in amazement as B.A.D., our white Schnauzer-Westie pup, sat looking at the cookie jar.

"Yep. Cookies. The only word she knows in English." Bob reached into the antique silver bowl that had become B.A.D.'s own personal best friend and commanded, "Sit, Bowie."

Of course, she didn't respond.

"*¡Siéntese,* Bowie!" Lucky for us, Bob's bilingual.

Down went the tiny bottom of our pup, her eyes glistening in anticipation, mouth open, waiting for her treat.

"*Buena muchacha.* Good girl!" Bob reached down, gave her the star-shaped dog cookie, and patted her head. He then handed one to Victoria with a smirk as I attempted to get the pup to sit for another treat.

Vic took a bite of the cookie. "Not bad, really. Tastes kind of like an animal cracker. Talking to a dog in Spanish, though, that's way over the top. I thought you were against bilingual education, Lieutenant Governor. And why do you call her B.A.D. again? She deserves that name, though. You need to get her some training."

I turned my attention away from the pup and back to my friend. "Her name is Bowie Aloysia Dog. But we call her B.A.D. or sometimes Bowie. We have to give her commands in Spanish. We got her from a Hispanic family and she's never heard English. Anyhow, Bob isn't the lieutenant governor anymore. No politics. Not now."

Exasperated, I continued with a sigh. "Back up. You were wondering about a Pandora's box and how that would relate to Bob? I need to figure out how this all fits together."

Vic's eyes widened as she licked the cookie remnants from her lips. "Yeah. You know what a Pandora's box is, right?"

I nodded in the affirmative. "Yeah. Like a mythological Adam and Eve thing. All the evil of the world escapes if you open it, like when Eve got the apple." I could feel myself starting to babble. Vic does sweets. I babble.

I kept on. "Yeah, didn't Zeus have a stunning beauty created with a deceptive heart and lying tongue? Yeah. Pandora—the first woman…then she got this box she was forbidden to open and, of course, she did. I mean what woman doesn't peek or open a gift, you know? In the box—well, it was really a jar—was all kinds of evil. Sorrow, plagues, but in the bottom, well there was hope."

Bob and Vic stared at me. B.A.D. was sprawled by the counter that held the cookie jar, sound asleep.

Bob gave Bowie a nudge with his foot.

"*Vaya fuera de muchacha.* Go outside, girl. Mama might be awhile with this one." She headed for the doggie door and I shut up. If nothing else, I can take a hint.

Vic took a gulp of coffee and leaned her elbows on the table. "You two aren't taking me seriously. I left a perfectly gorgeous man in my apartment, asleep, to drive over here in crappy weather, and you're talking Spanish to a dog. Not to mention the fact you're careless. You didn't even know your front door was unlocked. You've pissed me off enough to hurt you, so there's bound to be others. From your broadcast days, maybe?"

"Off the top of my graying head," Bob replied, " I can't think of anyone who's in jail. I nailed your lieutenant governor Jim Parsons with a few problem questions when I interviewed him a few years ago, and he's never forgiven me. Of course, the scandal surrounding my dropping out of the Michigan governor's race should have appeased him. He'll be the one taking the oath of office in a few days."

The mention of Jim Parsons caused me to shiver. Now there's one despicable man.

Vic was the first to react. "Yeah. Parsons. Amazing he's not in jail. Isn't moustache-chewing against some law? If not, it should be. And he lied about his credentials. I can't stand looking at that fat bastard." Vic was on a roll.

"When I was lieutenant governor of Texas I alienated some of the senators—Democrats—aw, shit." Bob's right hand landed firmly on his forehead, letting us know this light bulb moment was not a positive thought.

My own fears began mounting. Major coffee swig time. I turned towards Bob. "Gus and Marty, the senators—they're in jail along with Patricia, aren't they? And Glinnis is dead. Could the Pandora's box mean them? That someone wants retribution? Or could it be all the evil we uncovered about Parsons?" Damn. I was awake now.

Vic got up, refilled her cup, and returned to the table. "Back up you two—Glinnis was the lieutenant governor of Texas that was offed so you could get the gig, right? You then left office because of Gus and Marty—you wouldn't vote their way. Patricia, your former assistant, or whatever, is locked away. Sounds like someone's bigtime pissed at you. And then there's Parsons." Victoria's breathing slowed down, her complexion returned to its natural shade of ivory, and the sweat disappeared from her upper lip. She appeared relieved that we'd figured out who might want to harm Bob.

Me? Totally freaked out. "Stop! No one is going to hurt Bob. They're in jail, okay?" My voice raised a full two notes higher in pitch as I stretched out my hand in protest.

B.A.D. must have felt the tension because she gingerly walked back through the doggie door and curled up in the corner.

Picking her up, I tried to ease her apparent fears. "Don't worry, sweetie. No one's gonna hurt Papa. He's going to teach at the college and give speeches. We'll all live here and be just fine."

Bob smiled and took the pup in his arms. "Forget it, Beth—she doesn't understand English, remember?"

"I hate it when you call her Beth," Vic blurted. "She's been Chrissy her whole life. Her name is Christine Elizabeth. Your using her middle name is controlling. That's what I think. It's controlling."

My patience was beginning to fray. "Okay you two. This is stupid. Pick, fight, squabble. Let's finish off this coffee, calm down, and figure out why you're here, Vic, and what you have to do with this, Bob."

Vic rolled her eyes again. "Yeah. Caffeine always calms me down." If nothing else, my best friend is facially expressive.

Placing his coffee mug on the table, Bob tried to keep Victoria on track. "From the top, are you exaggerating this at all?" He's normally a patient man, but Victoria's sense of drama sometimes interferes with reason.

"Nope. Texans are the only ones with a true gift for exaggeration." Her stern look made the words sizzle as she spoke them.

Bob's shoulders slumped; apparently accepting this was one battle he wasn't going to win. "Okay. You made your point. However, I don't know a Minnie or a Benny. The only people I know in jail are duly accounted for. I'll check with John about Blane and any dirt he might have on him. Lord knows if there's dirt involved, John will know. In fact, he called my cell phone and left a message yesterday. He's coming over later this morning. At a more respectable hour." Bob finished off his first cup of coffee and headed across the kitchen for a refill.

Vic turned toward me, her back to Bob. "You're Catholic. Isn't there something about people in purgatory being able to be between here and there? Like they can come and visit you or something?" Victoria's sudden interest in religion was amusing, considering she is so willing to share her sex life in Technicolor.

I was stumped at this turn in the conversation. "Are you talking about spirits? Where are you headed?"

"Well, Margaret's not been dead all that long. Maybe she's stuck somewhere and is coming back to haunt you. I'll bet she's talking to us through the Hot Scot. That's what I think."

Irritated, I sighed a response. "Please, Vic, have some respect. She's been gone less than a year." Bob wasn't married to Margaret when she died, but she was the mother of their son. The pain was still real.

Standing up, Victoria headed through the great room. As she opened the heavy wooden front door, a blast of cold swept in. Her cat eyes squinted. "Thanks for the coffee. I guess I'm not being taken seriously."

She picked up the wreath that had fallen off the door and threw it inside. As she turned to go, she shot Bob an agitated look and volleyed her parting shot. "Listen up, Larken, I don't care whether or not you believe what I've said, or in ghosts. But trust me, Hell hath no fury like a woman who's dead."

CHAPTER 2

Courage is not the lack of fear. It is acting in spite of it.
—*Mark Twain*

Victoria's hasty exit left me shell-shocked. "Guess she made her point. Do you think we treated her like she was some bimbo who couldn't tell reality from a dream?"

Closing the door, Bob turned back and held my gaze. "Well, there was no love lost between Margaret and me, but bringing her up like she was a ghost set on destroying my life—that was way out of line. Let her cool off some."

"Good idea, hon. She did creep me out, though. Maybe we should have taken her more seriously. She's colorful, but she wasn't making up that dream."

Going back for another cup of coffee, Bob added, "Man, I'll bet she was a handful when she was a kid. She's obsessed with your name. Why is she so upset that I call you Beth instead of Chrissy? Seems strange to me."

"Oh, she's so protective. Might be a control issue. She's always been a big sister since Mama died. We were five—and she's been the only person ever since who thinks they can control me. Daddy spoiled me, Vic tried to control me. She might be jealous of you. When you changed my name, it took some of 'me' away. Pisses her off. She's so touchy about names."

Bob sat there and listened, without a sound, as I continued.

"I think the name thing started in kindergarten. The first day of school the teacher told us to raise our hand when our name was called. I guess the parents put their kid's nicknames down on the paperwork. She went down the list—Chrissy Pullen, Randy Rawls—of course Vic's name, Wexford, was last. When she didn't raise her hand, Mrs. Sullivan asked why. Vic told her she hadn't called her name and continued to tell Mrs. Sullivan that her name was 'dammit.'"

"Holy shit—keep going! This is so Vic." Bob grinned as he waited for me to continue.

"Her folks always said 'Dammit, hush!' 'Leave that alone, dammit!' She thought that was her name. It got her crying that first day because the kids laughed at her."

Bob smiled and shook his head. "That proves my case for mandatory and state or federally subsidized early childhood education. If she'd gone to a quality preschool, she would've known her name, dammit."

I smiled as I pushed aside my empty coffee cup. "It's all about politics with you, isn't it, Larken?"

I took his stare to be an affirmative.

We sat there until Bob broke the silence. "Well, as much as I'd love to sit here and listen to my wife tell kindergarten tales, we should try and figure this out so Vic can regain some semblance of sanity. I'll see what John knows about Blane MacGowan. All I know about him is based on rumor."

That caught my attention. "Such as?"

"He's good-looking, loves his whiskey, and wears a very long kilt in those Scottish parades. Men laugh at him. Women pant. That kind of thing. Oh. When he was a judge, he was known for putting away anyone whose morals were in question sexually. Talk about a dichotomy."

Motioning for him to join me on the couch, I placed my hand on his thigh and responded, "I was in high school—maybe just starting college—but I remember reading about some judge up north who partied by night and prosecuted by day. He loved to hang women out to dry after he'd been shafted. I take it that was Blane. Wasn't he the one that attorneys would follow the night before a case? If he had a good time, they felt certain their case would be handled fairly and if not—goodbye client?"

"Yep. That's Vic's Hot Scot all right. Women and whiskey. Then his dad died and he and his brother decided to take over the distillery."

It was coming into focus for me now. "Easy way out if you're up for reelection and have dirt under your bed."

"Great analogy, Beth. That's why I hired you in the first place—you have a way with words."

When he smiled, I noticed the crow's feet had started to emerge around his sparkling blue eyes. The stress of the past year, I presumed. The gray at his temples made him appear distinguished. Same thing happened to Daddy after Mama died and he got grayer every time business took a downward spiral. Now the vice president of process engineering for Ford Motor Company, Daddy proudly sported a full head of salt and pepper.

I grinned. "Always knew Daddy's tuition dollars would pay off somehow. I'd say he's gotten double his money's worth. A daughter who works for a politician turned professor and a fabulous son-in-law."

"Now don't you start tellin' tall tales, lil missus. You know your daddy worries about me. I'm a Texan, fifteen years older than his baby, a former politician, and a former broadcaster. All of those qualify me for lower than Texas red dirt in Frank Pullen's eyes."

I shot him a coy smile. "Aw, c'mon. Just because you were born and bred outside of Michigan doesn't mean you're as twisted as the Rio Grande. Almost, but not exactly."

Bob gave my rear a slap. "Glad to see you've finally learned some Texas geography, but you've gotta lie some, darlin. Don't you know that if you can't tell a lie you'll never amount to anything in Texas? Yep. That's an almost direct quote from the late John Connally. Another great Texas politician. He's a lot like me."

I knew there was more so I asked, "How's that, hon?"

Without missing a beat my broad-shouldered husband seemed to puff up as he said, "Handsome and shrewd with a strong belief that the most important way to address social problems is through education."

Seeing a glow come over Bob's face warmed my heart. No matter what happened, he loved the political world. It was in his blood, I guess.

Bob's eyebrows scrunched. "Wait! Were you even born when Connally was wounded and Kennedy assassinated?"

We both laughed. Bob would soon turn forty and I'd graduated from Michigan State just over a year ago. Math never was my forte, but that equates to a hefty chronological difference.

Sticking my nose in the air I huffed, "I know all about the motorcade. I read about it in U.S. history. Eleventh grade. Even saw the video. So there." I stuck out my tongue for emphasis and Bob took the cue.

"You wanna share that?"

Whenever Bob kissed me, I felt transported to a place only he had ever taken me. Meeting Bob Larken was one thing. Loving him was quite another. I had followed his career as a broadcaster during college and became somewhat obsessed when he was appointed the lieutenant governor of Texas. But the reality of being with him was even better than the fantasy. We'd been together nine short months, married only a few weeks, but it seemed as though we've known each other forever.

"I love you, Mr. Larken." I snuggled into his arms.

The peace was broken when Bowie jumped onto Bob's lap, a plastic bag hanging from her mouth.

Removing the Felspauch shopping bag from her tiny mouth, Bob laughed. "I see our little trash monster has been at it again."

"She's part schnauzer, hon. They're rooters."

"Rooters look for mice and other rodents, not plastic." Ruffling the curls on top of her head, Bob extracted himself from our cozy position and placed the pup on the floor.

Poking at Bob I chided, "Oh, aren't you the brilliant one. Not to change the subject, but what time is John supposed to come over? You forgot to tell me that little tidbit."

"Probably around ten. We'll fix some eggs, shower, and get a fresh pot of coffee going before he gets here. Fair enough?"

I pouted. "Yeah. I was hoping we could go back to bed for awhile."

"Back to bed or back to sleep?" With that, Bob kissed the top of my head, picked me up from the sofa, and carried me upstairs.

"Bob? Beth?" The voice boomed throughout the house and sent B.A.D. flying down the stairs, barking louder than a rottweiler on patrol.

"Forgot to lock the door again, didn't you?" I shook a finger at Bob. Men tend to go brain-dead when sex is involved.

Refreshed and relaxed, we threw on sweats and strolled downstairs to find Bob's dad, John Gaynor, smiling and holding B.A.D.

"Cute little thing. You should be more careful, though. All it took was the remaining bite of my donut to shut her up. She's an easy mark for a shrewd dog thief."

I shook my head at his attempt to chastise us. "We're in the middle of nowhere, John. I'm sure someone's lurking around waiting to snatch her up. Grand Ledge is too safe for that."

"Please be careful. You never know."

Bob came to my rescue. "John, want some coffee? Come on out to the kitchen. Is it already ten?"

"Ah. Newlyweds always lose track of the time." He smiled and sat down at the breakfast table.

"When you left the message on my cell phone, you did-n't say what's up."

"Can't I just come over to say hi?"

I knew better. It wasn't like John to call and want to drop by. There's always a reason.

Fixing two cups of vanilla nut coffee, I offered John cream and sugar, then placed a small, snowman-shaped plate of date bars on the table. "Obviously, you had a donut on the way, but we can munch on these." I pulled out a chair, sat down, and braced myself.

Bob reached up and got a mug from his special cabinet. My dad gave me mugs from all of his travels and they'd now become Bob's favorites. This mug was square with the face of a catfish on the front.

"This is bigtime ugly but it'll do the job." Bob filled the mug as he shook his head.

Smirking at Bob, I said, "There's actually a brotherhood of catfishermen. You know Daddy and his weird facts and holidays. That mug is from one of those moments. He was in Florida one year during the Florida Catfish Classic."

Bob joined us, moving his chair closer to the coffeepot. "Glad to know that. Maybe we can give this back to him for National Catfish Day or something. I'm sure there must be one."

"Children, children, children." John's eyes shone and he smiled as he looked at Bob, then me.

John tapped his cup with a spoon before clearing his throat and speaking. "Well, I talked with the Secretary of State yesterday. I like to catch him on Mondays. Always in a good mood after going to church the day before. I know these things."

Since the past is just a prologue to the present and future, I felt certain John knows all sorts of juicy tidbits. I sensed that a bomb was about to drop, so I decided to be the one to ask, "So, what's the news in Lansing these days?"

John continued. "The Secretary assures me that the elections commission won't bring to light that although Bob was a registered elector when he announced his intention to run for governor, he wasn't exactly a quote, qualified elector, unquote per Section 22, Article 5."

I was confused. "What does that mean, exactly?"

"It means that his eligibility could come under attack. If he hadn't dropped out of the race when Margaret was killed, the legal entanglement might have been enormous." John looked at Bob, whose silence had me stumped.

I needed to hear Bob's story. "Did you know you weren't qualified?" I took a deep breath and braced myself.

"Well, no. I wouldn't have made the announcement if I thought it was a problem. This is the first I've heard about it. John, did you know?"

"That article did come to mind. I believe the way around it is due to the fact that you are, indeed, registered to vote here. Have been for years and years. Since you were in grad school and bought that place in the Upper Peninsula as an investment. Now, as for being a qualified elector…"

I'd had enough. "Can you explain to me what a qualified elector is, please?"

Bob returned to his silence as John explained. "You need to have lived in the state for the four years immediately preceding the decision to run. But, there is a caveat. You can leave the state for however long you wish as long as you had the intention to return. That is where I had explained that you always wanted to return to Michigan and live in the cabin up north."

Bob sprang to his feet and yelled, "You did what?"

"I explained to the elections department that you most assuredly had intended to make Michigan your home. That's all." John shrugged his shoulders in a who-cares fashion.

"What gave you the right to speak for me? That is not the truth. I was living with Margaret and our son in Texas. I was the lieutenant governor, for God's sake."

My head hung down and I whispered a silent prayer to Saint Denis, the Patron Saint of strife. Seemed to be the best choice for this occasion.

"Sit back down," John commanded. "It's over. Done with. Parsons is about to be sworn in and you can teach and do news broadcasts. Parsons would like to talk with you before the inauguration, though."

I knew this was going to be a crappy day. Awakened at six, dumped on at ten.

Bob closed his eyes. "Parsons? What does *he* want? He's the governor-elect. Got what he wanted. This state is sure to go to hell within the next four years. I'm so glad I'm officially a homeowner and resident of Michigan now. Great investment." He blew air out of puffed-up cheeks and finished off his catfish mug of coffee in one huge gulp.

My temples pounded and to make it worse, I'd forgotten the name of the saint that covers headaches. "John. Thank you for covering Bob's ass again. No. I don't really mean that." I found it tough to stand up and speak my mind around men—always had. I let my father decide things since Mama died. Lately, I'd been letting Bob and John tell me what to do.

With inner strength about to hit the boiling point, I dug in my heels. "I don't like the way you always run interference for Bob. You have dictated his career and life. That might have been fine when he was with Margaret but it is not okay now. I want a normal life. I don't want to have to look over my shoulders wondering if I'm being watched, or fear for my life when I have a cup of coffee. Is it poisoned?"

Standing up and heading for the back door, I proclaimed, "The choice is quite easy. From now on, consult us before you manipulate our existence. You two can keep talking. I'm taking a walk."

Unfortunately, I'd forgotten to put on a jacket, hat, or gloves. Not a smart choice for the first week of January in Michigan. I'd left empty-handed so that ruled out getting in the car and driving off, as well as going down to the barn to sit and think. The car and the barn were locked, with the keys to both neatly tucked inside the zipper pouch of my purse. My haste to escape confrontation was not one of my brighter moves. I'd done this before. You'd think I'd learn.

Walking down the snow-covered trail to the riverside, I propped myself up against an oak tree hoping that the dense woods would shelter me from the chilling breeze.

Instinctively, I repeated the words to a poem I'd written years before. The Grand River winds through the MSU campus and during a particularly down moment I penned my thoughts.

> *River come and take me away.*
> *Release me from life's tragic play.*
> *Sweep me in your ebb and flow*
> *To a place I'd never think to go.*
> *River come and take me away.*
> *Make me forget the trials of today.*

I don't exactly know why I feel the need to retreat when times are their worst, but I do. This was one of those moments.

The snow masked the sound of his boots, but I could hear Bob rubbing his hands together. Looking back through the trees, I saw my husband walking toward me.

"Beth? Beth, please. Don't do this. John means well. He's known I'm his son my entire life. It can't have been easy watching me grow from a distance once I was adopted."

"I know, but it's not just you now. It's me. It's your son. Dave is a junior in high school. Now, more than ever, he needs to see a united front. Strength. Dave's mother is dead! I entered into the picture before she was even gone. We have to deal with that head on. I don't want John interfering anymore!"

"Dave will be fine. I think our decision to keep him in Austin was the right one—he's so involved in speech and debate. He was here for the wedding and for Christmas and he'll be back over spring break. We'll go down there to see him once Parsons takes office and I've shown the party it's a united front."

I knew that was all true. Bob and Dave had two great weeks together over the holidays. It hadn't been easy for Bob to make the decision to let Dave stay in high school with his friends down in Austin, but father and son kept in touch constantly by e-mail and phone, and Dave seemed happy in his familiar Texas world.

Bob looked at me and continued. "I'm out of politics, so no harm will come to any of us. Never again. John was just letting us know that the Secretary of State—"

"See? John wanted to let us know. The Secretary of State should have let us know. John is right smack dab in the middle again. I won't have him dictating my life. I just won't!" This newfound strength was foreign to me, but I knew it was the only way I could find peace with all that was happening.

Bob put his arms around me for warmth. "C'mon, lil girl. Let's get you warmed up. John said he got the message. He's left."

Why do I always end up melting when he turns on that Texas twang?

"I'll make you a deal, Larken. I'll go back with you if you build a fire to take off the chill."

"I'll take off more than the chill, darlin'."

Feigning disgust, I pursed my lips before saying," I'm still upset that John pulls all the strings. But you promise it's over?"

With a wink, Bob responded, "Normally a politician is known by the promises he *doesn't* keep."

I resigned myself to his truth. "I guess that says it all."

CHAPTER 3

Those who cannot remember the past
are condemned to repeat it.
—*George Santayana*

All of a sudden my life felt like someone had put it in a blender and hit the oscillate overdrive button. Beaten, chopped, frappéed, pulsated, and puréed. First, a perceived threat concerning Bob; then a scandal surrounding his aborted bid for the governorship. Another shit-happens day in the life of the Larkens. All without my consent or knowledge. Totally unacceptable.

My mental gymnastics were soon cut short by the sound of B.A.D. barking at a fevered pitch. Running into the great room, I spotted Bob stoking the fire. The pup was jumping up and down like a bunny on Easter morning. With a grin on my face, I scooped her up and shouted over the yelps, "What does she think those flames are going to do, attack her?"

"I suppose. You'd think by now she'd know nothing was gonna happen. Then again, she goes berserk whenever the vacuum comes out, too." His tone was flat, his face expressionless.

No time like the present to bring up a sour subject. "We never had a chance to mention Blane MacGowan to John. And what's this about Parsons wanting to meet with you?"

"I don't know, Beth. You had your hissy fit and walked out before we could find that out. John wasn't about to stick around for more hormonal fireworks."

"I'm finally getting a backbone and you're upset? You used to love my spirit and encouraged my independence. Now they're a detriment to your relationship with John? Great vote of confidence. Thanks."

I was not gaining points. Bob turned away from me and headed upstairs.

"Don't walk away from me, Bob. Don't you dare! We need to iron this out. Right now!" My latest rant apparently fell on deaf ears. I decided to take the typically female way out and capitulate. I was determined to do it by my rules, though.

I dialed John's cell phone. If he screened his calls, I must have passed the test. He picked up after one ring.

"John, can you come back out here, please? I'm sorry I was so stern but I really think we need to talk some more."

After a few throat-clearings, he said it was okay.

"Appreciate that, except Vic was over earlier and mentioned a Blane MacGowan. Bob thought you might know him. Vic was worried because he talked in his sleep about Bob."

More throat clearing. He finally declined the invitation, explaining that he had some end-of-year meetings. He assured me that Blane was harmless.

I tried to sound chipper, but my inner voice told me not to buy into this latest tale of harmless behavior. "Okay, maybe you can come out once the New Year has been rung in and we have a new governor."

The call ended and I walked up the stairs making my mental plan of attack. Deep breath. I remembered a prayer Mama use to repeat.

> *All-powerful and ever-living God,*
> *You choose the weak in this world*
> *To confound the powerful. Amen.*

Make that a double amen!

I snuck up behind Bob and whispered, "Hey, you. I called John and we'll get together after the first. We're fine. He has to know that your life—our life—isn't up for an Oscar and he's not Director of the Year."

Turning around, he placed his arms around my waist and gently kissed the top of my head. "You're right. Maybe he's trying to make up for lost years."

"He's been doing this your entire adult life, though. He made sure you got that first broadcast job. From then on, whether you knew it or not, John was instrumental in the twists and turns of your public and private life. We have our own lives now. I want him to be a part of it—I just don't think he needs to orchestrate it."

Squeezing me tighter, he looked down at me, a seriousness coming across his face, a gentle blend of love and concern. "I guess I never really thought it out like that. Damn."

He extracted his left arm from around my middle and looked at his watch. "Let's go have a sandwich at the Log Jam, pick up a few things in town, and you'll still be able to make it over to Lansing in time to meet with Shelly."

Shelly Parsons. Jim Parsons' wife. A saint in my book. I was going to meet with her at the Olds Building at four. She was getting her office arranged, meeting with her staff, and going through the normal transition from wife of the lieutenant governor to her new role as Michigan's First Lady. The Olds Building is a secure facility, so we'd have the freedom to talk openly. In a weak moment, I'd agreed to meet with Shelly when she called out of the blue a few weeks ago, but I had no idea what she wanted to talk about. Anyone married to a jerk like Parsons had my automatic sympathy, that's for sure.

Bob lifted my chin and smirked. "You went silent on me. Dangerous. I can help ya out if ya wanna be dangerous. Close your eyes."

He kept one arm around me and guided me through our bedroom. We stopped. Hearing the balcony door open, I shivered as we walked outside. I heard a *whooooooooosh* and I immediately knew he'd turned on the outside heat lamp. Damn. I love it when we argue and make up. Opening my eyes, I noticed that Bob, at some point, had swept the snow off the balcony. He didn't like it piling up on the wood. Pressing me against the wooden railings, Bob showed me how sorry he was that we had argued. I most definitely accepted his apology.

Walking back into our room, I shook my damp hair. "Let me do a quick make-over and we can leave. Give me thirty minutes?"

"I'll change, too. I'm ravenous now." There was the wink.

His wink always disarmed me and I couldn't help but laugh. "I have a tough time staying mad at you, Larken. I'm trying to get over that, but this way is much more fun." I gave him a quick peck on the check and retreated to the bathroom to transform myself from vixen to virgin. Okay. Maybe that was a stretch.

Driving into town, we passed Felspauch Food Center. "Hey, we should stop in the market on our way home," I said. "We don't have any champagne to usher in our first New Year as husband and wife!" I don't normally drink. When I do, it's not a pretty sight but you can't ring in a new year without some bubbly.

Bob snorted, "Yeah. You and champagne. This should be interesting."

"Quit it! I'll only have a sip."

Stopping at the next traffic light, he said, "Promise? I don't want a snoring, slobbering blob lying next to me the night before Parsons takes the oath. Too much of a reminder of what we're getting as governor."

"Ewwwwwwww. You think he snores, too? Can we change the subject? We're about to eat." Laughing about Parsons was about all we could do at this point. He was an easy target for jokes and ridicule.

A quick left and then right into the parking lot and we were ready for lunch. The Log Jam is a local spot, warm and rustic. You always see someone in there you know. Today was no exception.

Bob walked up and extended his hand to the owner of the Four Seasons Gift Shop. "Hey, Ken, who's tending shop? You leave it up to the lovely missus again?"

Returning Bob's handshake and giving me a hug, Ken responded, "You got that right. This time of year it's a zoo. So, we called a business meeting. Just finished. I'll take her back something, though."

I smiled and laughed. "Nice of you. What kind of business, monkey business or game reruns?" I poked him in the ribs. "We were headed to your place after a quick sandwich. I want to make a basket filled with your special soaps for a friend."

"Always have plenty of those. I'll make sure Kathy sets some aside for you." His smile was warm and his tone, as always, upbeat.

Bob, looking around, said, "I see a table just waitin' for us. Get back to work, Ken!" The friends shook hands again before we retreated to a place in the corner.

We ordered the special Log Jam Sandwiches and devoured them without conversation. The steak was medium well with the mushrooms, onions, and cheese spilling out the sides.

Brushing the final crumbs from my lips and wiping the juice from my chin, I spoke. "You can stay put and have a beer if you want. I'll run around the corner to the shop and get the soaps."

"Good idea." Bob smiled. "Every time we go into that store, you end up conning me into buying half of what's there. Go get the soaps and we'll be on our way."

"Not a problem. I won't let Ken talk me into anything this time. Promise."

That was one promise I didn't keep. Skulking back into the restaurant, I spotted Bob sitting and chatting with his best friend, David Hawthorne, more affectionately known as Thorne. They'd known each other since grad school. Thorne had built our house, one log and stone at a time, with his bare hands.

"Hey, you two!" I called.

Thorne stood as soon as I greeted them, walked over, and gave me a bear hug. "Hi, kiddo. Happy New Year, almost. What have you got in that bag, or should I say bags?"

Bob shook his head. "I knew it. Ken should win the best salesman of the year award. He could talk a Texan into buying a Yankee flag, I'm tellin' ya. Hard part is he's so dern nice and everything in his store is first class."

Taking a bag from me, he peered inside. "Well, there are the soaps. Enough to keep the entire Midwest clean."

A hearty laugh escaped as he reached for bags two and three. "Ah. Cookbooks. Are you going to turn into Betty Crocker now? This scares me. I remember some of your more famous dinners—burnt popcorn, scorched soup, and a side of brick brownies."

I gave him a good smack on the head with bag number four.

"The cookbooks are for Jill, you louse. Great sale and you know how she is with cookbooks."

Jill was an assistant for Bob back in Texas. What a cook. We'd planned to make her the chef to the governor had Bob become the number one man. No way would she want the job now. There's not enough money in the state's budget to feed Parsons.

"Well, maybe you could keep one for yourself? Is there a cookbook for those who can't cook, maybe? One of those apprentice type things?" Bob appeared to be enjoying this banter. Thorne knew better than to join in. Sometimes it's more fun being an observer.

I stuck out my lower lip and feigned being hurt. "Okay. See if I make you coffee tomorrow morning."

"Pout away, brat girl. It adds to your charm." With that he snatched bag four from me. "Now these I like. We gonna frame them for the study?"

He had extracted dozens of postcards depicting the historic sights of Grand Ledge. Some looked like oil paintings, others like charcoal sketches.

"Thanks for spoiling my surprise, Larken. That's what you get for being nosy."

Turning to Thorne he responded, "She called me nosy. Me? Nosy? She's the one who can't wait until Christmas for her gifts. I found out from her dad that she peeks and snoops, so I put enough tape on the gifts to keep out Houdini."

Thorne, in his laid-back manner, replied, "Smart, Larken. Now give her back the bags." He turned toward me with a smile. "It's nice to see you two so happy after all that's happened. Well, I've gotta run and split some more firewood." Standing up, he continued, "Do ya need any?"

Bob kept the bags, pulled me to my feet, and smiled. "I'll carry the bags. It's the southern gentlemanly thing to do and, yes, we could use another cord. Thanks, bud."

The two shook hands and embraced as best friends do. I stood back, enjoying the sight. Thorne turned and gave me a kiss and whispered in my ear, "Take care of your hubby. Parsons' inauguration won't be easy to swallow."

Nodding in agreement, I watched Thorne leave, waving at everyone as he passed. Quiet, gentle, strong, and loyal.

Poking at Bob, I said, "Don't forget to stop at Felspauch for the champagne and maybe some more chew sticks for Bowie."

Bob smiled. "I think she'd rather chew the grocery bags, but we'll get some rawhide anyhow."

Once we were back in the car, Bob exclaimed, "Damn. We didn't put Little Miss Fluff Puff in her kennel."

"Oh, she'll be all right."

Bob sighed. "Easy for you to say. You weren't the one who left the date bars on the table."

We finished at the market and made a beeline back home. Fortunately, the main roads weren't too icy for this time of year. The city acted swiftly to salt the highways, but the private road into our subdivision is another story. Slowing down, Bob focused on the many twists and turns that wound between our barn and the main house.

I looked to the right and exclaimed, "Bob! Stop! Look at those tire tracks. Someone's been here."

Bob slowed down and stopped at the entrance to a clearing that led to our barn.

I looked down at the ground and visually followed the line of the tracks. "Those weren't here when we left. I'm sure of it. I glanced over towards the barn as we passed by on our way out, thinking how festive it looked surrounded by the evergreens. Right off of a postcard."

Bob glanced at the small building Thorne had built. Its architecture was that of a traditional barn, but it was a complete apartment inside. He looked back and forth between the main road and the clearing. "You would have had to look over me. I don't think, from that angle in the car, you could have seen the ground."

"But we're the last house on this road. The tracks aren't ours. We haven't been to the barn lately. We'd better check, okay?"

Once out of the car, Bob walked ahead of me. He followed the tracks until they abruptly stopped. "Looks like whoever it was got out—there's footprints."

The snow flurries had melted, leaving muddy tracks behind.

I glanced around and noticed, in a bare spot between the trees, a cigarette butt. "Look at that," I said as I pointed toward the white butt, which would have blended in with the snow had it been earlier in the day. "I don't like this."

Bob continued his perusal of our land. "Looks like they backed out almost directly over their own tracks. They didn't turn around. No way to tell where they went from here. The main road's been salted. Probably some kids that sneaked out for a smoke."

I wrapped my arms around myself. "Make that kid. Only one butt, unless they shared."

Bob could see me shiver, even though I was dressed warmly. "Hon, Vic's way off base. No one is out to get me. We're fine."

I wondered if he was trying to convince himself, or me. "I still don't like it, and you still need to think more about someone who's named Benny or Minnie or Bernie or whatever the hell she said."

Bob grabbed my hand. Silently, we walked back to the car and headed farther down the road to the house.

As we climbed the steps to the front door, we could hear frantic barking. Bob fumbled nervously for the right house key.

Shaking my beret-covered head, I mumbled, "Fine time to have locked the door, but I don't think she's inside." My heart raced faster as the barking became louder. "Oh my God, I think she's somewhere outside. Listen!"

I started to walk around the front of the house, following the growls, when I spotted Bowie, covered with mud, front paws out, rear end in the air. She was growling at the trash can she'd knocked over. Soiled napkins, used paper plates, and discarded plastic forks were strewn about the side yard that runs between the kitchen and the woods.

Bob walked closer. "Settle down, girl. *Coloque abajo.*" He hung his head. "I guess I forgot to lock the doggie door this time."

I scooped her up, hugging her close despite the filth. She shivered but didn't stop growling. "You also forgot to latch the trash can lids. I know your mind's been preoccupied with the wedding, getting ready for the new semester, and all of the speeches and lobbying you're doing for the environment, but you really have to be more careful." The newly discovered irony made us both laugh.

Bob sat on the ground and commented, "Wow. Here I am taking up arms for Michigan's ecology—my dog's a litter pup and . ."

He stopped mid-thought. His eyes fixed on one clump of waste. "Beth, go inside. Take B.A.D. with you and stay there."

"What . . ."

"Just do it! Now!"

As I turned to leave, I saw him kick away a half-smoked cigarette.

CHAPTER 4

Throughout history, it has been the inaction
of those who could have acted; the indifference
of those who should have known better; the silence
of the voice of justice when it mattered most
that has made it possible for evil to triumph.
—*Halle Selassie*

Bowie and I went upstairs and waited for Bob. When Bob yells, or barks out a command, it's for a good reason and not to warm up his vocal chords. I went over the events of the day and wondered if we should call the police. What would they do? No crime had been committed—other than littering. I doubt they would consider two cigarette butts a big deal. But when you add in B.A.D.'s barking and Blane's dream . . .

By the sound of the heavy-footed climbing, I knew Bob was pissed. He was a formidable six-foot-four, but normally very light on his feet. This thudding was not a good sign.

My husband stood in the archway at the top of the stairs with his arms crossed. He looked down the hall into our room and shouted, "Beth, you're goin' to see Parsons' wife, right?"

Walking towards him, I noticed his clenched jaw and his chest rising and lowering from heavy breathing. "Yeah, I'm supposed to be there around four. I should leave pretty soon. Everything all right down there?"

"Sure. You go on. Be careful." His tone was flat; his eyes had lost their spark. "You might also ask Shelly where that husband of hers has been all day—if he's been out or had any appointments. You're good at that. Finding out shit without folks knowing you're bein' nosy."

No smile accompanied that last comment, which was not like Bob. Not like Bob at all.

"You okay, honey? Maybe we should stay home."

"We? I'm not goin' to help out Shelly. No way."

I grinned. "The 'we' is the pup and I. You look like you could use some rest. Let me go and live vicariously through her."

Turning and walking down the stairs Bob asked, "Vicariously?"

"If you hadn't taken yourself out of the race, the job of Michigan's First Lady might have been mine."

"I thought you didn't *want* me in politics. Now you regret not being First Lady? I can't win."

"No, no, no. I just feel sorry for her. She must have been devastated when she found out her husband is a con artist. She has her own private hell. The least I can do is help her out some."

"Oh, do tell why, Beth. Makes no sense to me." Bob had plopped down on the sofa in the living room, shoulders slumped, legs spread.

"John was determined to put you on the ballot and make sure Parsons didn't run. He had that dirt on Jim for years and kept silent until it would do his cause—you—the most good. More manipulation."

Bob snapped. "It's still a secret. He'll be our governor and that's that. Go on, but be careful."

"You think someone is really trying to harm us?"

"I meant to be careful because of the snowstorm that's brewin'. That's all. There's sand and a shovel in the trunk."

Unconvinced, I still smiled back. "Sand? Shovel? No way. I get stuck, I call you."

I tripped as I approached the couch to give him a good-bye kiss. I wondered how on earth Bob could think someone who bumbles and fumbles over her own two feet could dig her way out of a snowdrift. I write, play the piano, pray, and babble. I don't shovel.

Recovering from my slip-and-slide routine, I grabbed B.A.D's pink sweater off the couch and scooped the pup from the floor. Not a trace of dirt remained.

Bob stood up and escorted us to the door. "Remember to keep her on the leash when you're in the building. We don't need her to land in puppy jail for trashin' our First Lady-elect's office."

"Gotcha." As we made our exit, I called back to Bob, "Don't forget to take some time to figure out who you might know in jail, okay?"

He just waved back.

Once on the main highway, it was a straight shot to Lansing. As I turned onto Saginaw Highway, I could see the dome and all of the festive holiday lights and decorations. Snowmen, Santas, dreidels, and banners reading "Peace on Earth" in various languages had transformed downtown Lansing into a sea of multicultural décor.

Turning onto Michigan Avenue, I made an immediate right into the Olds Building parking garage where the executive offices are located. I showed my identification, smiled for the camera, and parked in a reserved spot. Wasn't *my* reserved spot, but the lot was fairly empty and surely I deserved something for coming out during the holidays to help the wife of my husband's nemesis. I love it when I can justify illegal behavior.

I snapped Bowie's pink leash onto her collar and we hopped out of the car.

"Come on, girl, time to strut and put on your good manners."

As we went up the elevator, I took one final deep breath. Although I did like Shelly, her taste in husbands was suspect. Physically, she was lithe yet voluptuous, a natural blonde with gorgeous huge eyes, and she possessed the kindest spirit you'd ever want to encounter. For her sake, I hoped there was more to her husband than meets the eye. He was rotund, balding, smoked like a fiend, and was addicted to Pepsi and those disgusting diet cookies. He chewed his moustache when he was nervous, which amounted to most of the time. He brought his lower lip up and raked away at the hair and then went over to one side and chewed. Not a pretty sight. While repulsed, at times I caught myself feeling sorry for him. It can't be easy being in his position.

I noticed the only open door was the soon-to-be office of Shelly Parsons. I didn't need to announce our presence. Bowie did that with one dainty yip. Shelly came to the door wearing a big smile, casual black slacks, and a black cashmere V-neck sweater. The black clothes made her pure white teeth sparkle like the Christmas lights that still adorned the building.

She greeted me with one of those political hugs and kisses—a gentle squeeze followed by a kiss to the air by my right cheek. "Hi there, Beth. It's really wonderful to see you."

Looking at Shelly, I felt thrilled that she would be presiding over all of the State dinners. This gal had style. "It's good to see you too, Mrs. First Lady almost."

"And you brought the pup. She has really grown since I saw her last!" Of course, B.A.D. was nothing short of perfect. She sat there and gazed up at Shelly with her huge eyes wide open. For a change, B.A.D. was not living down to her name.

Shelly patted Bowie on the head. "You can take her off the leash. I'll shut the door. She'll be fine."

All I could think was, *Yeah. Right.* But I unleashed Bowie anyway and she immediately trotted over to the burgundy wing-backed chair, jumped up, and sat there as if she were trained.

Shelly took some pictures from a box and placed them on her new mahogany desk. "So, how were your holidays? How's David John?"

I noticed she didn't ask about Bob.

"Christmas was great, although it was tough on D.J. You know, losing his mom, Margaret, in such a tragic way, then his dad moving from Texas to Michigan . . ." I hung my head. Tough didn't even come close to how it was on D.J. He tried to buck up, but the holidays are meant for family. No matter what I do to keep things light, I am not his mother.

"I'm sorry, Beth. When will he go back to Austin?"

"He left the day after Christmas. How about your holidays?"

"Oh, we had so many events, and now the transition and inauguration. The boys, I think, got short-changed. They're used to limelight, but this is so intense."

Her eyes grew larger as she exclaimed, "Wait! I nearly forgot! Congratulations, Mrs. Larken!"

"Thanks. I'm so glad the church was free on the 19th and that it all worked out so beautifully, so close to the holidays and all."

"December 19th. That's right. We had the holiday party for our new staff that night. I'm sorry we couldn't make it. I've heard it was absolutely breathtaking."

The holiday party was a convenient excuse. The truth was, they weren't invited.

Shelly sat down atop her desk, an elegant pose. Almost picture perfect. "I read that you wore your mother's gown.

How special for you. And your dad had a wedding vest! I didn't know there was such a thing."

"I don't know that there is, but Daddy has a vest for everything. He had it made especially for our big day. He took a linen tablecloth of my grandma's to the tailor. He's such a sentimental slop."

Shelly laughed and continued, "Well, I really am happy for you. A bit surprised you had a Mass but. . ."

"Oh! Bob turned Catholic so we could have a wedding mass. Father Tom was so understanding."

Shelly grimaced and said, "That was awfully quick."

"So much has changed. It's not a long, drawn-out process anymore. Father Tom explained it all and helped get everything in order."

Smiling, Shelly got right to the point. "I don't suppose a sizable donation from John Gaynor hurt."

"I suppose not. Well, we need to get to work."

We sorted through boxes and sifted through books and knickknacks, attempting to make the staid surroundings more inviting, and talked more about the wedding. My journalistic mind had a question brewing and I decided to let it pop out. "Shelly, do you know Blane MacGowan very well? Or anything about him?"

"Oh, I know bits and pieces. He was a judge a few years back. His dad died and he and his brother inherited the family distillery. It's a good business but they've always struggled."

I remembered Vic's stories about his incredible apartment and souped-up car. "That's strange, he sure lives high off the hog for someone who struggles."

"Guess some folks spend it even if they don't have it. He's quite a looker. Maybe it's an entire persona he feels he needs to live. I remember reading a profile on him somewhere. He went all through school on financial aid and academic scholarships. Bright man. But, between you and me, I think he lives beyond his means. Why do you want to know about MacGowan?"

"He's dating my best friend and I always like to find these things out. I'm pretty protective where she's concerned. Lord knows she needs it." With that we both laughed, easing into a comfortable routine.

She kept busy while continuing to talk. "There was some hint of scandal but it was rumors and whispered comments."

"Really? Like what? I mean, if it's not confidential."

"Oh, nothing ever came of it. Just talk. I tend to hear about college chums of Jim's a lot." She let out a sigh.

"Blane was a college buddy of your husband's?" I was shocked.

"Sure was. I guess he put away a lot of women the last week before his father passed away. Maybe from the stress of his dad being in the hospital so sick. But any woman picked up for solicitation got the slammer. Might have also been because of Governor Melvin. He had a real crusade going, and cleaned up Lansing's red light district. I guess MacGowan was showing his support. Good PR move, politically."

"I suppose. What were the rumors, though?" Now that I'd discovered her information came from the inside, I was even more curious.

"One older gal, her name was Robin. She got prison time. Keys thrown away. I remember her name because everyone said, 'MacGowan locked up the state bird!' It was a joke around here. She even had wild reddish hair. No one could figure out why the harsh sentence, and the next week he was off the bench."

"Wow. Poor old gal."

As we started in on the next box, Bowie jumped down from the chair and growled at the door. We turned to see the door open. In walked the governor-elect.

"Bowie. *Silencio.*" I guess my pronunciation was off because the guttural sounds continued.

As Jim Parsons passed Bowie, he looked down and said, "Nice to see you, too, dog."

She must have felt he wasn't sincere because as Parsons bent over to pick up a box of books, Bowie sprung in the air like a rabbit and nipped his rear. Well, I hoped it was his rear—surely B.A.D. couldn't do much damage to Parsons' ample behind. But the noise Parsons made—a shrill howl that made it sound like he'd been attacked by a herd of coyotes—wasn't a good omen. Apparently, Bowie had nipped the governor-elect in the parts I really didn't want to have to think about. Shelly ran over to help her husband and I picked up B.A.D., who was definitely living up to her name.

I tried not to laugh, but seeing this huge beast of a man gripping his privates was almost too much to take. "I am so sorry. I don't know what got into her. She has her shots, I swear she does."

Shelly tried to calm her husband down, and then eased my fears. "There's no blood. So much for the pants but he'll be fine. It's okay."

This brought out a groan. As Parsons looked up from his bent-over position, I could see the veins protruding on his forehead. "Okay like hell! First Larken tries to castrate me politically, then he sends his dog to do it personally. There's a damn leash law, you know."

Bowie had found another target. The trash can. She knocked it over and rummaged through it with a vengeance.

"Honey, I told her to take the puppy's leash off. It's my fault, really."

I had to respond somehow. "I really am sorry. Please. Replace your pants and send us the bill, will you?"

Another moan. "Damn straight I will."

As Shelly guided her husband to the chair previously occupied by B.A.D., she said soothingly, "Oh, no need. Really. It's all right."

"We'd better go. I'm so sorry."

Parsons glowered at me. "You always cause trouble. Go somewhere and pray. First MacGowan and now you."

With that final comment ringing in my ears, I re-leashed B.A.D so there wouldn't be a repeat performance and asked, "Blane MacGowan? What about him?"

Parsons closed his eyes. "This is not the time to discuss a private visit with an old friend. I'm dyin' here."

"But. . ."

He cut me off before I finished. "Just go!"

Pup on leash, we headed for the garage. Someone had ticketed the car. Talk about a crappy day turning crappier.

CHAPTER 5

Lady Astor to Winston Churchill:
"Winston, if I were married to you,
I'd put poison in your coffee."
Winston Churchill to Lady Astor:
"And if you were my wife, I'd drink it."

Before pulling out of the parking garage, I shoved the ticket in the glove box and said a quick prayer to Saint Clare of Assisi for good weather. A snowstorm would do me in.

No way did I want to cook dinner, so I swung through the A&W near the house. Great comfort food. Plus, they know me. When they see the pup, they give her a small bag of fries.

Luckily Bob had, once again, forgotten to lock the front door. With my hands full of food and holding onto Bowie's leash, finding the right key for the door would be a trick.

Imitating Fred Flintstone, I let out a "Honey, I'm home!" as I let go of the leash. Bowie scrambled in, dragging her pink restraint as Bob rounded the corner.

Eyeing the bags of food, he said, "I missed you two, but I really am happier to see the hot dogs!"

Grabbing the takeout he gave me a kiss on the forehead and asked, "Any excitement at the capitol? How's the transition coming along?"

Extracting the yellow slip of paper from my purse, I handed it to Bob and mumbled, "Here ya go. Consider it a pay-back for your pup biting Parsons."

"She what? A ticket? Oh, this had better be good." Bob sat down, tore open the fries, and gobbled away.

I felt the babbling starting to boil but couldn't hold it back. "See, Shelly told me to unleash her and she was being really sweet and we were having a great time till Bowie started to growl. Well, she was growling away and Parsons walks in. He bent over and, well . . ."

My tale was cut short by Bob's hearty laughter. "Don't tell me. She bit him on the ass. This is choice."

"Oh, it's only choice because you weren't the one humiliated. I about died on the spot. But I did find out some more about MacGowan."

"Hold that thought, hon. Is Parsons okay? Damn. I can see the headlines now . . . 'Governor-Elect Bitten by Has-Been's Bitch.' Will you write up a rebuttal press release so we have it on hand?"

He was smiling but maybe he was serious. "He's fine. Don't think he'll be breaking any bed slats in the near future, though." The very thought made me feel somewhat sorry for him.

A root beer belch replaced Bob's laughter. "Now that I've found out Bowie has neutered our new governor, what's this about MacGowan?"

"Apparently, MacGowan went on a rampage before he stepped down from the bench. Locked up a bunch of women for solicitation. Shelly specifically remembered one named Robin. Does that ring a bell?"

He shrugged. "Nope. I was in Texas at the time so it didn't matter much to me."

"Ah. All right. Makes sense."

Bob tilted his head, looking at me quizzically. "What's all this obsession over MacGowan? Vic overreacted to a dream. He probably had too much of his own whiskey the night before."

"Call it a journalistic sixth sense. I don't know. There's something nagging at me. Plus, I found out MacGowan visited Parsons earlier today. I wonder what that's all about."

Passing me another hot dog he replied, "Forget about it. Parsons and MacGowan go way back, and Vic can handle herself. Frankly, she can handle herself and a dozen men. Next time you see her things will have calmed down. Trust me."

I sighed, "Last time you told me to trust you I signed an agreement to keep silent about our relationship."

Holding his head erect he retorted, "Confucius say, 'Silence is the true friend that never betrays.'"

"I'm not so sure. That silence betrayed me several times. It's time to break that silence and find a life of our own."

"Who made you Little Miss High and Mighty all of a sudden? Is this life so terrible?"

Pushing my unfinished dinner aside, I sat there, quietly thinking what I should and should not say. "I'm not high and mighty. I'm just ready to start a life that isn't dictated by other people."

"Life is give and take, hon. To get something you normally have to give something up. It's just the way it is. You got me. You got this house, and a pretty damn easy life. A little silence for a lot of perks. I'm goin' upstairs to read."

He retreated and I stayed behind, staring into the swirling snow outside the windows.

Normally, I would have followed and apologized for being a brat. This time was different. I tidied up the kitchen, unlocked the doggie door so Bowie could let herself in and out, and walked into the great room. Sitting down at the piano, I drifted off into another world. Music has always comforted me. Now was no exception. I began playing the *Moonlight Sonata*, the song that drifted through the night air when Bob and I met on Mackinac Island. I was reminded of the magic we both felt from that moment on. It also reminded me that Bob was married at the time, and that I soon found myself swept up in political corruption and cover-ups. We signed papers when Bob divorced Margaret and agreed to live in silence. No one would ever know we married ourselves; Margaret, in the eyes of the world, remained his wife.

Breaking out of the melancholy refrains of Beethoven, I let my resolve move into a piece I'd been writing in my head over the past few months. Unlike Beethoven, this was written in a major key, without the undertones of sadness found in *Moonlight*. The crescendoing strains and variation flowed with ease. The acoustics of the great room were tailormade for this music that serenaded my soul. I needed to begin notating what I had written but, for now, I played it from memory.

I heard the stairs creak under the weight of Bob's footsteps. "Beth, that's beautiful. What's it called?"

Continuing the next passage I answered, "*Mattinata.* That means 'morning song.' Like a new beginning."

Bob sat across the room as I finished with a trill and final chord. "Bravo! Encore! What does the title mean again?"

"Morning song."

"That's as close as you'll ever get to anything even remotely resembling a morning." He smiled, gave me a wink, and clapped for my creation. "Brava, brava!"

I stood and curtsied. Joining him on the window seat, I said, "You know, it's wonderful having something that is completely mine. No one can dictate the music to me. It comes from my heart. It's all mine."

"You've written press releases and PR material, too. Don't shortchange yourself, girl."

"But those were for someone else. This music is for me. Big difference."

"You'll still write for me, won't you? I don't mind you playing around on the piano, but I really need you to help with my speeches and PR."

I looked him straight in the eyes. "What speeches and PR, Bob? You're teaching two college courses and haven't given a speech in months. When you do, you're much better at extemporaneous speaking. That's your forte. Speaking from the heart. Just like I compose from the heart. It's the same—you with words and me with notes."

His eyes squinted as he questioned, "You're quitting your job as my assistant?"

I smiled and shook my head in disbelief. "You're kidding, right? I thought you fired me and I just helped out here and there. I didn't know it was a job, per se."

The ringing of the phone cut short our conversation. Jumping up, and glad for the interruption, I answered on the third ring and heard Victoria's voice. No time for pleasantries. The ranting began immediately.

"Vic, calm down. He'll come back. Does he normally leave a note?"

I motioned for Bob to come to the phone. Placing a hand over the receiver I told him, "Blane left. When Vic got home he'd split. She's a mess."

I continued the conversation. "Vic, hon, it's late and the weatherman called for snow. Blane'll be back. Stay put. He'll call. Get off the phone and leave the line open, okay?"

She took me literally and hung up.

Placing the phone back on the cradle, I scratched my head. "She was really over the top."

Bob placed his arm around me and led me back to the couch in front of the fireplace. He placed fresh logs on the smoldering embers and poked at the timber.

I continued to ramble. It's a stress thing. "She got back from our place and he wasn't there. She thought he'd just gone out for coffee but she noticed he'd made and finished off a pot at the apartment. He normally rinses out the pot and puts whatever dishes there are in the dishwasher. He didn't do that. And as soon as she walked in she noticed the smell of cigarette smoke. Blane quit smoking a while back."

"Could he have had someone over? Someone who smokes? Can't be that hard to figure out. Not many folks smoke nowadays."

"I don't know. I listened to Vic and didn't have reaction time."

Bob, going into investigative journalist mode, questioned further. "So Blane had quit smoking, but the place reeked of smoke. He hadn't left her apartment like he normally does when he visits. Sounds to me like he had someone over and they left in a hurry."

"Wait! Parsons smokes and, when I was at the capitol, he said he'd seen Blane today. Maybe that's who it was. But that still doesn't explain why Blane left without a note or a call. Vic has a cell phone."

"It's too late to do anything about it now. Tomorrow you can call Shelly and see what kind of cigarettes her husband smokes and that will answer one question. By then Vic may have heard from MacGowan anyhow."

"I don't know. Vic was really concerned because of the smoke."

"If it would make you feel better, we can drive over to Grand Rapids tonight. Tomorrow we can stop in to see John on our way back here. If you don't get out of the house, I might lose you to the piano. Deal?"

It sounded like he was trying to be concerned for Victoria, yet something about his tone wasn't sitting right with me.

"We wouldn't even get there until midnight. And tomorrow Daddy is going to come over."

He smiled one of those cockeyed grins and wiggled his eyebrows up and down. "Are you saying no to a night in a motel room with me? That's a first."

"Well, when you put it that way, I guess it would be an adventure. We need to find a place that takes dogs, though, and I should call Vic."

I called Vic back while Bob retreated upstairs to pack. Bowie roamed between the kitchen and the bedroom until it was time to go.

Bob picked up the pup's bowls, favorite toy, and blanket. I put some dog food and treats in a plastic baggie and grabbed a covered bowl for water on the road.

Laughing, Bob commented, "It's not a cross-country trip, hon. We're only going to Grand Rapids."

"What if we get stranded in a snowstorm on the way? You have a flashlight in the car, right? And blankets, just in case? Oh, and don't forget the cell phone adapter and matches."

"Matches? Are we going to send up smoke signals to the highway patrol if we need help?" His chuckle disarmed me.

"Stop already. I don't want to get into trouble along the way. Where's your gun? Do you have a permit to carry a concealed weapon in Michigan?"

"Now I know you lived in Detroit too long. You just sit with Bowie in your lap and pray. That should keep us on the right track." His comment was accompanied by a quick smack on my rear as he placed the pup in my arms.

"Wait! Where's her sweater? She can't go out without her sweater!"

"Calm down, girl. You're obsessed. I think you're O.T.T."

"You mean O.C.D.? Obsessive compulsive disorder? I am not!"

"Nope. I said 'O.T.T.' Over the top. You're definitely O.T.T. Geeeeeez, if you're this bad with a dog, what on earth would you be like with a baby? "

I plopped down on the couch with a mighty thud. "Now we're talking babies? I thought we were going to stick with a puppy? When did we decide on a baby?"

His eyebrows went up and down again. "We didn't, but we can work on it."

"I think the idea of a motel has gotten to you, Larken." I stood back up and, with Bowie under one arm and my favorite pillow under the other, left the house. I made sure Bob locked up this time.

The weather held, with only a few scattered flurries. "I should have one of those books that tells you what hotels accept pets. How will we know?"

"We won't, but if it's a plain old motel with the doors on the outside we can sneak her in. We'll just be there to sleep."

It was my turn to wiggle my eyebrows. "I'll remind you of that later, Larken."

Bob pulled into the first decent motel inside the city limits, which was a few minutes from Vic's. The motel was filled to capacity. Four motels later I lamented, "See? I told you we needed to bring blankets. What if we can't find a room?" I closed my eyes.

"Who's the saint this time?" he inquired.

"Raphael. You know—one of the archangels. He's the saint for travelers. Well, Christopher was, then they ousted him. Raphael also is the saint for nightmares, which this is and . . ."

The ringing of Bob's cell phone interrupted my liturgical babbling.

Bob laughed, "See? There is a God."

"Answer the phone!"

"Hi Vic . . . I knew it was you from the readout!"

After several "uh-huhs" and an explanation of our plight, Bob said "thanks" and hung up.

"What did she want?"

"She wondered where the hell we were. Said to come right over."

"No way. She only has one bedroom and Blane gave her a kitty for Christmas." Bowie's moan reminded us that staying with a cat was not an option.

"She'll take the couch and we can have her room. She'll crate the kitty. What's the cat's name again?"

"Pookie. Isn't that cute?"

"If you say so. Bowie, brace yourself. Here we go."

Several turns later we were in front of Vic's apartment complex, a colonial-style building surrounded by what would be, in the spring, gardens. Bob carried in our bag and all of the dog paraphernalia, and I gripped Bowie tightly under my arm with a fair amount of apprehension, since she'd never been around a kitten before. You just never know.

Ringing the bell to gain admittance, I turned to Bob. "Go easy on her. She hasn't lost a man in a while."

"Who said she lost a man? He didn't leave a note. He didn't call. He didn't leave, he was just inconsiderate."

The buzzer went off, the lock clicked, and we walked up to Vic's place, the back left apartment on the second floor.

Opening the door, Vic hugged me, then Bob, and removed Bowie from my arms. "Come meet your cousin, Pookie."

I briefly hesitated before speaking. "You think that's a good idea? She's never been around a kitten. I thought you were going to crate her."

Bob placed our bags on the floor and waited for the pup's reaction. At first she whimpered. Then she cowered between my legs as the kitten approached. The kitten pounced and Bowie peed. Typical.

"God, Vic, I'm so sorry." I got paper towels from the kitchen and mopped up the mess. "Do you have any pet neutralizing spray? I don't want this to leave a smell."

"I have at least a gallon left. This hasn't been the easiest cat to introduce to the litter box." Vic returned with the spray bottle and the pets settled into a routine. Bowie ran and Pookie chased not far behind. Orange hair fluffing out, her unusual blue eyes gleaming, this kitten was a powerhouse.

Ignoring the pets, Victoria frowned. "Put your things in the bedroom and then we can get to work figuring out why he left." She burst into tears.

Bob wasn't used to tears. I pout until I get my way. No need for tears.

Wiping her eyes, Vic went into the kitchen and returned with an ashtray filled to the brim with butts. "Look. Look at all these cigarette butts. He told me he quit, but look!" Her hands were shaking and several fell to the floor. Bowie quickly ran over to investigate.

"No!" Bob reprimanded.

Looking at Vic and me, he explained, "Those can be lethal for pets. Pick those up, okay?"

I scooped up the mess and placed one of the butts in the pocket of my sweater. Vic placed the ashtray on top of the television and commented, "Well, one of two scenarios. Either someone was here visiting him or he took up smoking again. I asked all the neighbors and no one saw anyone coming or going. Not even Blane. Alice next door is a nosy bitch. She knows and sees everything. Not this time." Vic sighed, " Just when I needed her, she lets me down."

I put my arms around my best friend. "We'll figure this out. Let's get some sleep. He's probably just pissed that you left so early. Did you leave him a note when you flew out of here this morning?"

Hanging her head, Vic admitted, "No."

"Let's sleep on it," Bob said. "It's been a long day. We need to have clearer heads to figure this all out."

Vic trotted over to the couch and mumbled, "Okay, I suppose you're right."

Wiped out from the stresses of the day, Bob and I said our goodnights, kissed, and crawled into Vic's bed. It didn't take long for Bob to conk out. I propped two pillows under my head and listened to the dueling snores of Bob and B.A.D. They needed to synchronize their nasal passages. I nudged them both, vowed to get a good pair of earplugs, and drifted off to sleep.

Chapter 6

Silence is the virtue of fools.
—*Francis Bacon*

"Okay, time to rise and figure out who's after Bob." Victoria, once again, had awakened us.

I covered my ears. "Don't you ever knock?"

Bob responded, "At least she's wearing clothes this time."

Two early mornings in a row. Damn.

Victoria turned and walked to the bedroom door. "If I waited for the two of you to get out of bed, we'd never get this solved. I'm trying to save your ass, Larken. I guess you'd rather wait for the bloodshed."

Vic exited and slammed the door. Looking towards Bob, I said, "So much for sleeping in."

Bob kissed me on the forehead. "So much for sex."

I thwapped him with the pillow and headed for the shower.

Bob followed closely behind, pulled on a sweat suit, and said, "I'll take Bowie out to do her business, then shower and dress."

We finished our morning routine and met Vic in the kitchen. A fresh pot of coffee and a plate of sweet rolls sat on the table.

I began the investigative routine. "Vic, I didn't see any used matches in the ashtray. Would Blane have a lighter with him?"

"I don't think so. But if he had cigarettes stashed somewhere, maybe he had a lighter, too. Or maybe he went out and bought cigs and a lighter."

As he turned his attention to Vic, Bob chimed in, "Do you have a lighter?"

Vic walked to the counter and opened the drawer under the phone. "Yeah. I keep one in here to light candles during blackouts." She looked inside. "Yep. It's still here. I don't think it's been moved because it's tucked under some scrap paper."

I continued the questioning. "So, either Blane was smoking or someone was here that does. We know he met with Parsons. We don't know where. Bob, Parsons wanted to meet with you, too, right?"

His elbows placed on the table, his chin resting in his left palm, he replied, "Yes ma'am, according to John, that's right. Hope it doesn't mean if I meet with him I disappear." A smile crossed his face.

"Get me some paper and a pencil, Vic. Let's write this all down."

She complied and I made a list of what we knew. "Seems to me we need to skip over to Lansing and see how Parsons has been spending his time. Ask a few questions. Vic, you stay here in case Blane returns. If you do have to go somewhere, take your cell phone. I tried earlier. When you didn't answer, I was a mess."

She shrugged her shoulders. "Like I said, I forgot it. I was a mess, too, ya know. You can be in Lansing by lunchtime if you leave soon."

Bob called the capitol and arranged for us to meet with the governor-elect. I packed and took Bowie for a short walk.

Once in the fresh air, my mind went into hyperdrive. The quagmire of recent events made me wonder how far-reaching the arms of deception go in the world of politics. Daddy had warned me to beware, but, as usual, I hadn't listened. I needed to figure out why I felt so uneasy concerning Blane's alleged disappearance. We had just touched the surface, I feared. Was it a dream? Or had the demons of a more sinister realm come to surface in his sleep? And what did this have to do with Bob? I avoided the icy patches of ground as I returned to Vic's apartment.

I buzzed for admittance. While standing outside, I heard voices coming from several of the units. If there were a heated discussion between Blane and a visitor, one of the neighbors might have noticed. Maybe they were accustomed to noise and blocked it out.

Vic buzzed for us to enter and Bowie let out a yelp. Vic's neighbor opened her door an inch and peeked through the crack. We were greeted by an elderly woman donning a button-up housecoat and blue fuzzy slippers. Her silver hair was knotted on top of her head like a cinnamon bun.

She glared at me, then looked at the pup. "This is a 'no dog' apartment building, missy."

"I'm so sorry. We came for a brief visit and are leaving right now." I extended my free hand. "My name is Beth. I'm Victoria's best friend." My overture was met with silence. "I wonder if you heard any commotion yesterday morning? Maybe two men talking loudly or doors slamming?"

She pursed her lips. "I don't make it my business to intrude in other people's lives. But I did hear a lot of coughing at, oh, about eight I'd say. Yes, it was eight. I know it was because the seven a.m. news was ending and it's an hour show."

"Did you hear anything else, ma'am?"

Before she could answer, Victoria's door opened and Bob came into the hall with our bags.

"Bob, I'd like you to meet Victoria's nice neighbor. I'm sorry, I didn't catch your name."

She put her nose in the air. "You didn't catch it because I didn't throw it out. It's Alice. Mrs. Alice Dunbar, but Mr. Dunbar is dead. Passed about five years ago now."

Bob said, "I'm sorry, ma'am. It must be hard on you." He poured on the Texas drawl that women love.

Alice took the bait. "Oh, that's so sweet of you. If you're not in a hurry, maybe you'd like some tea? I always have the kettle going." She melted visibly as she looked at him. The same way I melted the first time he spoke and the same way every woman reacts when he talks and pours on the Southern charm. Damned unnerving.

Bob continued his cunning ways. "Why thank you, ma'am, but we need to head over to Lansing. You take care of yourself. Next time we're in town we'll visit, if that's all right with you." He smiled and extended his hand.

She ignored me and shook his hand.

Alice Dunbar returned to her apartment and Victoria joined us in the hallway. "You two let me know what you find out. Want some coffee for the road?"

I answered, "Me? Turn down coffee? Never. Thanks."

Vic reached behind the door and retrieved two Styrofoam cups of steaming coffee from the end table. "I knew you'd want it. Anything else?"

I handed Bowie's leash to Bob. "Why don't you take the pup and the bags to the car? I'll be there in a minute with the coffee. I need more cream."

He kissed Vic, they exchanged brief good-byes, and Bob headed for the exit. What I wanted were a few tidbits from the apartment.

"Vic, have any Baggies?"

"Sure, why?"

"I want to take the lighter. I have a cigarette butt in my sweater but I've contaminated it. I want to use a Baggie to get a new one."

"What the hell are you doing, Chrissy?"

"I don't know. But if Blane doesn't come back . . . "

Her voice about pierced my eardrums. "If he what? Oh my God."

"I don't think anything happened to him. These might not be his butts and I want to be sure no one else used the lighter, that's all."

Vic's face turned pale. "I'm not leaving here until I hear from you, so you'd better call. Now you have me all worked up."

"Have you tried his cell phone?"

"Hell yeah. Voicemail is picking up the calls. He turned it on when he was here so we wouldn't be interrupted, you know?"

I knew.

"So, he might have forgotten to turn it off. That's all. It's not been very long."

Vic protested. "Almost twenty-four hours. When can I report him missing?"

"Missing from what? The cops would laugh at you, Vic. Calm down. We'll check around some and then tomorrow, if you can't reach him, call his brother. That makes more sense. Right now both the cops and his brother would view you as a hysterical broad who got dumped."

Wrong thing to say.

"I am *not* hysterical and he would *not* dump me!"

"Whoa, Vic. You came to us because you thought Bob was in danger. We have to assume he still is. Or someone is. So stay put, okay?"

Vic slumped and sat on the floor.

All I heard, as I walked out the door, was Vic mumbling, "Shit, shit, double shit."

CHAPTER 7

You never know what a fool you can be till life gives
you the chance.
—*Eden Phillpott*

As Bob and I entered, governor-elect Parsons stood in
the hallway and watched the movers clear out Governor
Stan Melvin's files and mementos by the boxful. We saw
Lydia, the current governor's assistant, stationed outside
the executive office at her usual desk. Her "What part of
NO don't you understand?" plaque remained on its corner.

Lydia spotted us and said, "No transition team is going
to move me until Parsons takes the oath of office. Until I
hear those final words, 'So help me God,' I'm not going
anywhere. Stan Melvin is still the governor of Michigan
and I'm still his assistant."

Bob approached her and beamed. "Nice to see you,
too, Lydia."

They exchanged a hug and mumbled a few words. I
tapped on the plaque. "You going to bequeath this to your
successor? I think she'll need it."

"No joke. Well, I'm not about to speak ill of the man
voted into office, but your husband was my first choice."

Bob perked up. "Hey, wait! I thought Thorne was your first choice? Remember, I'm a married man now." He poked her in the ribs and kissed me on the cheek. I got the best of the deal.

Lydia grinned. "I was talking about the governorship, smartass. I hope Dave and I can take a vacation once I'm out of a job."

I placed my hand on her shoulder. "You two both deserve it. All the work you did here the past eight years, and then helping with the wedding. We both really appreciated that. You and Dave were amazing. Time for the happy couple to regroup. I tried to aim the bouquet towards you, but Vic, well, you know how she can be."

We both laughed. "Yeah. I have a bruise where she shoved me!" Lydia said.

Jim Parsons approached, smirking. "So sue her."

Bob looked at the soon-to-be governor. "Funny as ever, Parsons."

"I believe you're here to see me, Mr. and Mrs. Larken. Sorry for the mess, but I'm sure you remember what it's like during the transition phase. Excuse us, Ms. Mayer."

We nodded at Lydia, who grimaced in return. We walked into the newly elected governor's office. I hung my head, and said a quick one to Raphael the Archangel.

"Larken, I see your wife's still at it."

I snapped, "Hush!" and finished out loud, "May all our movements be guided by your light and transfigured with your joy."

I glared at Parsons. "That was for a happy meeting. So let's get on with this. We have a few questions."

Bob interrupted, "Jim, before we get down to business, well, sorry about our pup. Don't know what got into her. We left her in the car this time."

Parsons brushed his hand through the air. "We didn't want any more kids. Saved me a ton of money for the surgery."

We laughed and sat down on some straight-backed desk chairs. They were all that remained from Governor Melvin's tenure.

I wanted to get the Blane stuff out of the way. "Let's get right to it. You saw Blane MacGowan yesterday, right?"

"Sure did. He swung by here before going on vacation."

In unison, Bob and I exclaimed, "Vacation?"

"Yeah. Said it was spur of the moment. Just some time to be alone. Guess the whiskey business was wild, with the holidays and all. He wanted to take a few days off."

"Where was he headed?" Bob asked.

"Don't know. I asked him and he told me he was just gonna drive and figure it out. He seemed tired. Sleepy."

Bob and I looked at each other and nodded our heads in the affirmative.

I noticed a lack of ashtrays in the office. "Don't they allow smoking in the executive offices? I thought you always smoked in your office when you were the lieutenant governor."

"Tryin' to quit. I'm using those patches. Not easy, but I believe the good folks of Michigan deserve a positive role model." His chest puffed up, and he held his head high.

Bob looked at Parsons and said, "Good for you. That's a great start in your governorship. Very admirable."

I continued with the questions. "Did you go anywhere out of the area yesterday, or have any other visitors?"

"What's this third degree all about? You sound like a cop. Are you writing an article on 'What our new governor does during the transition?'"

"No, it's more personal. Blane is dating my best friend and she thinks he's missing."

Parsons grinned. "She get dumped again?"

Bob replied, "No. She didn't get dumped. He apparently forgot to tell her his vacation plans or she wasn't listening when he did."

I shrugged my shoulders, "That's probably it. She has a tendency not to listen when the subject's not entirely on her."

Parsons grumbled, "To set the record straight, I was here all day. I visited with Blane. I also visited with Gaynor. He came by to discuss money, as always. When he left here, Gaynor went to talk with Stan. Or that's what he told me. That was it. Now, I have a question for you, Bob."

Parsons went to the credenza and opened a large bottle of soda. Non-diet, of course. He poured drinks for Bob and me. "Ma'am?"

"Thank you, governor."

"See? You Texans aren't the only ones with good manners. Speaking of Texas, you goin' back anytime soon, Larken?"

"You wish. I might just stay here to keep my eyes and ears open. We made a deal, remember? Your past and lack of credentials stay buried. In return, you consult with me on educational issues and push through the adoption legislation. We need to have insurance companies pitch in or pay the medical bills for biological mothers. Their insureds are paying maternity coverage, why can't the bio moms use it? The costs of prenatal care are absurd. That's what prevents many adoptions. It's also why so many celebrities and wealthy folks can adopt and why so many others have to go into debt to become a parent. It's sick."

Bob was on a roll. "Adoptive parents have to pay legal fees and the fees for the biological mother's health care. On top of that, you promised to rally against what I term 'biological blackmail' . . . birth parents requesting and getting fees for all sorts of things. They cover it up by calling it 'reasonable living expenses' but you and I know what goes on. It's basic economics. Supply and demand."

He hesitated and I said, "See, Bob? You don't need a speechwriter. You know exactly what you want to say."

"It's all true and I'm passionate about this. You know that."

Parsons turned toward me. "If he doesn't need you anymore, does that mean you're available?"

I choked on my recent swig of soda. Bob jumped to his feet and smacked me on the back. "Nice way to get back at us for the dog bite, Parsons. Make my wife choke and give me a damn heart attack."

I assured them I was fine and inquired with a smirk, "What did you have in mind, Mr. Almost Governor, sir?"

"I had an idea. You're young, spirited, and could give a fresh look to the upcoming administration."

"Wait a minute, Parsons. You called us here to steal my wife? I might not be in politics at the moment, but I'm hardly dead."

The way he said 'hardly dead' made my stomach flip. The thought of Bob and death . . .

"Hold on," Parsons interrupted. "No one's writing your political eulogy. I want her to put in a year building a positive image for my administration."

I grimaced. "Bob, you're out of politics. Governor, you're offering me a job? This is a joke, right?" No one laughed.

"No joke. I'm offering you a job. Every time I do something positive, every brilliant comment I make—I want you to be the one responsible for getting those sound bites heard statewide."

"This would include your pro-adoption stance?" I asked. "Your education initiatives? Bob would do the behind-the-scenes work. He'd scout it, you tout it, and I spout it?"

They both laughed. "Larken, she's got what it takes."

Bob smiled. "Why do you think I offered her the job after reading one article and knowing her a mere three days? She's talented and charming."

I stood and curtsied. "Is there going to be a duel? This could be good."

"Parsons, she'll be hell to live with now. And no, she's not for hire."

That pissed me off. "Excuse me, when did you become my agent? If I want to work for the governor, I'll work for the governor." To soften my anger, I batted my eyes. I didn't want to embarrass Bob in front of his nemesis.

"You two need some time to talk this over?" Maybe Parsons had changed. His voice, still smooth and low, was also softer than it used to be.

"That's a good idea," I responded. I did need time to think this over. It was a huge decision. "When can I let you know?"

"Well, I'd like to name my entire staff within the first week of being in office. Sound fair to you, Mrs. Larken?"

"I suppose. And thank you for the offer. It's quite a compliment."

"Which brings me to you, Larken. Think you'd like to head my Department of Education?"

Bob shook his full head of soft hair. "*Your* Department of Education? I believe that's *Michigan's* Department of Education. For a minute I thought you'd changed some, Parsons. It's still all about you, isn't it?"

"You knew what I mean. Still on the edge, hey? Calm down. You've got something I need, and I owe you. You're the only one that can drive home a positive pro- gram for the kids of Michigan. I want our educational system to be the role model for the other states, Larken. You've got what it takes. Progressive ideas and a positive plan. Unless you plan to take it back to Texas."

"What are you getting at, Parsons?" I smelled a rat. An overgrown rat with a moustache.

"Seems to me I heard the Secretary of State discovered a slight problem. Something about you weren't eligible to run for office here in Michigan? To think you were always going to return to your beloved Michigan. But wait—you were the lieutenant governor of Texas! A born 'n bred Texan. Seems like I heard you say that, didn't I?"

Bob sprang to his feet and headed toward Parsons. "Hear this, you lowly son of a bitch, you better keep that . . ."

"Stop!" I protested. "Both of you, stop!"

I walked over to Bob and grabbed the hand that was positioned to strangle the yet-to-be-sworn-in governor. "Bob, let's go. This isn't the time."

He yelled, "Isn't the time for what? Politics? Keep going, Parsons. What about my aborted run for your job?"

"Like I said, Larken, you were not qualified to run for the governor of this state. You failed to meet the requirements of residency."

Bob laughed. "I failed to meet the requirements. Well, that's true. And you're qualified? You lied about your credentials, Parsons. If that tidbit hits the headlines. . ."

"Ah, but it won't now, will it. Old news in our battle for the dome. Seems we each have a little secret. But I'm about to be sworn in and you're not."

His pompous attitude reminded me why I always found him despicable. At first it was just his appearance and disgusting habits. Reasons to make a person's stomach turn but no reason for disdain. This was making me downright nauseous.

"Governor, what Bob did, or failed to do, is not illegal. He broke no law. The elections commission would have eventually figured it out and he would have been removed from the ballot. Not a felony. Not a misdemeanor." I placed my empty cup on the credenza and walked over to Bob's chair. "It happened so fast, his bid for the governorship. But it was not a deliberate lie. You, on the other hand, can you say you did not deliberately lie to the people you're about to represent?"

Parsons hung his head. "You made your point."

"Bob is not about to be arrested because no crime was committed. It wasn't good, I'll give you that, but it wasn't a crime." I wanted to break out in my own rendition of "Stand by Your Man." Instead I smiled, and placed my hand on Bob's shoulder. "Now, you need to excuse us. My father is coming over later today. I appreciate the job offer. It's a fabulous opportunity."

With that comment, Bob snapped his head around and glared at me. Looked like something Linda Blair would do in *The Excorcist.* "I think we need to talk. Now. Parsons, excuse us."

Bob grabbed my hand and pulled me through the office and into the hallway. No one was around so we talked in private.

"Beth, what the hell are you thinking? You can't be serious about working for that man."

"Let's not start, Bob. I just defended you in there. The real problem I have is not so much with Parsons as with John. Did you know he'd been up here yesterday?"

"No. He didn't mention it to me. I'm not his secretary, Beth. I don't always know where he is or what he's doing. Why?"

"Just wondered what business he had with Parsons. That's all. He was at our place at ten yesterday. He said Parsons wanted to talk to you. I'm just trying to get a timeline. Something's not right."

"I'll call him later. We've found out Parsons met with Blane and John and he's now on the smoker's patch. That rules him out as the one leaving butts everywhere."

"True," I admitted.

Reopening the governor's door, I peeked inside. "Sir, thanks again. You have some great ideas for a new, positive image. Sounds like something I'd like to work on."

With that, Bob swore. "Holy shit. This isn't happening." He stormed down the hallway and never looked back.

"I'm sorry, Jim. I'll call you."

Never in a million years did I think I'd be apologizing to Jim Parsons.

CHAPTER 8

Those who cannot remember the past
are condemned to repeat it."
—*George Santyana*

I slapped the DOWN button on the elevator. When I reached the main floor and rounded the corner, I spotted Bob.

"Beth, I can't believe you'd consider working for him. He was blackmailing us. We can't break free from this shit."

"My first question is whether or not we're staying in Michigan. You told me we were."

"Come on. I'm a Texan. I might want to go back there at some point. My son's there, for God's sake. I can teach here, but if something comes up . . ."

"So this isn't your home, like you spouted off when you were campaigning. It was just politics as usual, wasn't it. Anything for the power. Bob, you whored yourself. I can't believe we're having this conversation. Were you ever going to let me in on your plans?"

"Shit, what plans? I don't have any plans. I have thoughts. I have 'what ifs,' but nothing's a promise."

"Our marriage is."

He fell silent.

"When we got married you promised me we'd make a home together. I don't recall Texas being in the plans. David will be in college before we know it and have a life of his own. He can come here for summer and breaks. Remember? That's what we planned."

"Oh really? Did you bother to discuss that with D.J.? No. We made the decision for him. It's *his* life. *Now* who's being controlling?"

He turned and walked out of the building. The sound of his boots hitting the tiled floor rang in my ears.

I sat on a bench next to the security guard's podium, head in hands. Was I being controlling or was he? Did it matter? Damn right it mattered.

The doors automatically opened as I approached. He hadn't used the elevator to access the parking garage. Maybe he decided to take a walk and cool down. Easy to do in this weather.

Snow flurries blurred my vision as the wind whipped my face with a sudden blast. I worried about the sudden drop in temperature and decided to go rescue B.A.D. from the parked car. Luckily, we'd taken the truck, and had parked in the enclosed parking structure. The truck provided more protection against the weather than the convertible. Those cloth roofs were fine with the heater blasting, but parked, could get mighty chilly.

I entered the garage and noticed Bob was sitting in the truck with B.A.D., motor running. I opened the passenger door and, without a word, we traveled to Grand Ledge.

I needed to play the piano. I needed to pound the keys. Once home, the frustration that had built up over the past hour drifted from deep inside my soul through my fingers and filled the house with the rhythmic cadences of Bach and Beethoven, one melody after another. Over and over, purging my anger and fears. Bob sat and listened, his eyes gazing out the window. The Looking Glass River had long since frozen over. A few months earlier we'd gazed out that same window, watching canoe enthusiasts paddling from Lansing for a picnic. The river was now a scene of tranquil ice with a canopy of leafless trees.

"You feel better now? You really put your heart into your playing."

"I have to put it somewhere." I walked past my husband and started a kettle of water for cocoa.

He followed. "We need to talk about this. I won't work for Parsons. I will not lower myself to be a part of that administration. I'll give advice. I'll confer. I'll even demand but, by God, I won't take money from him."

"I might. I was thinking about it—about a job. I love my music and might try and do something with what songs I've written, but writing—image building . . ."

Bob's voice raised and he came closer, eyes wide, "Image building? Parsons? That would be two full-time jobs! Are you shittin' me? He's scum, Beth!"

"Man, you really do hate him, don't you? Look at it this way—it would be a great way to keep tabs on the inner circle. How else will we know if he's keeping on the straight and narrow behind the scenes?"

"You'd be a mole? Holy shit, I don't believe you're really considering this."

The phone interrupted and I looked towards Bob. He tossed the cordless handset to me and snarled, "I'm in no mood. Answer it."

It was John.

"Sure, come on over, John. Daddy will be here later. Why don't we all grab dinner? I've got plenty in the fridge . . . sure . . . okay."

I disconnected and tossed the phone to Bob. "That was your dad. He has something more to discuss with us. He's on his way."

"Oh, great. He never comes over with good news. Can't wait to hear *his* reaction to this offer from Parsons. I do want to find out why he met with the slime ball, though."

"Stop it, Bob. You're the one with O.T.T. Syndrome now. I think it would be great for me. It would keep me busy, give me something to do that I love."

"It's against my better judgment and wishes, Beth."

"It's not up to you. I would like your support but I don't have to have it. Isn't a marriage supposed to be supportive? If you want to go to Texas to do some broadcasts, that's fine with me. It's what you love, it's what you know."

Bob's eyes went from shooting daggers to the soft, gentle eyes of the man I'd spotted on the television a year ago. The man I loved. "We need to call Vic, too."

"Why? If she's heard from MacGowan, she'd have called, don't you think?"

"I'm worried. That's all."

"Well, wait till our dads leave. If we haven't heard by then, we'll give her a call."

"Bowie! Come here, girl. *Venido aquí, muchacha.* Whatcha got?" Bob walked over to the doggie door and pried open the pup's mouth. "*¡Mala muchacha!* Bad girl!"

"What's wrong? Is she okay?" I joined them by the door. Bob handed me a soggy, muddy cigarette butt.

He patted Bowie on the rear. "Scoot. *Enciéndase.* Go on now." She trotted away and laid on her pink blanket in the corner.

I looked more closely at what was left of the cigarette to see if it was the same brand we'd seen at Vic's apartment. It was too mangled to tell. "Bob, what's with all these cigarette butts? I've never seen them around here before."

"I don't know, but I'll ask John if Parsons smoked when they were together. Jim said he'd quit, and he didn't smell like smoke, but there's somethin' not right here."

"Nicotine is lethal for dogs, isn't it? Oh God, I hope she didn't swallow a cigarette. Should I call the vet?"

"Looked like she was just carryin' it around, hon. Keep an eye on her. She'll be fine. She doesn't usually eat the stuff she gets into."

The door creaked from the cold and we heard the stomping of boots. "It's just me."

We walked into the great room to find John, snow covered, shaking his head. "You two never learn. The damn door was unlocked again."

I reached over, took his coat and said, "We haven't been home all that long. Don't worry. Our attack dog is on duty."

Bowie sauntered into the room, stretched, and laid under the piano bench.

"I can see that. Bob, you do have a gun, right?" We all laughed.

As I hung John's coat in the closet, I noticed the distinct smell of smoke.

I suggested we sit in the kitchen. Bob lit the Franklin stove in the corner; we helped ourselves to cocoa and settled around the fire.

John put his hands around the steaming mug. "Great gathering spot. Cozy having that fire in the kitchen."

I looked past Bob and said to John, "You have a fireplace?"

"Sure. Can't imagine living in this weather without one. Of course, I travel a lot, but I use them in California and Texas, too. The nights get cold, you know?" His smile matched Bob's and they shared the same sparkling eyes.

I continued. "Sometimes I get so cold I keep my coat on when I sit around the fire. You know—until I warm up. Isn't that silly?" I watched John closely for his reaction.

"It must be a hormone thing. Wouldn't dream of sitting in a wet coat that long."

Bob looked at me and said, "Yeah. Must be a hormone thing. Spit it out, Beth. Whatcha gettin' at?"

"John, did you have this coat on when you met with Parsons?"

"Sure. It's my overcoat. I took it off and hung it over my chair. Why?"

"Did Parsons smoke at all when you were together?"

"No. He quit. Went on those patch things."

Bob turned toward John and asked, "Speaking of Parsons, what was that meeting you had with him about? We were there today and can you believe he offered my wife a job? Me, too, for that matter."

"He mentioned that. Interesting. Well, that's part of why I came out here."

I groaned and responded, "Oh, Mother Mary. This conversation is making me dizzy. Before we get to the gory details, I have one question. Who smokes?"

In unison, Bob and John blurted, "Huh?"

"John, I want to know who smokes. Your coat smells of smoke. It's not fireplace smoke. It's cigarette smoke. So, question is, who smokes?"

John turned pale and answered, "I do. Not much. Just every now and then. When I get nervous. Used to be a bad habit. Now it's just nerves."

Bob asked, "And why are you so nervous?"

"I was about to tell you before your wife, the self-proclaimed P.I., started her interrogation. It's about your mother."

Bob squinted his eyes. "What about my mother? She's been dead for years."

"No, not Martha. Your biological mother, Robin."

I jumped to my feet and yelled, "Robin? Bob's mom is named Robin? Oh geeeez. Don't tell me. She was a prostitute, right?" I pulled my chair closer to Bob and wrapped my arm through his. He remained speechless.

"Well, no, not really."

"Not really? You either are or you aren't. Last I checked you couldn't be a sort-of hooker. John, is that how you met her? Oh God."

"Well, not really. I mean no. I met her in San Antonio. She was a barmaid. A gorgeous one at that." His eyes twinkled with the memory. "She had the glamorous job of swinging over the bar. Know what I mean?"

"I'd rather not have the details. Is she the Robin that MacGowan locked up? How did she get from San Antonio to Michigan, of all places?"

Bob shook his head and muttered, "Shit."

"Go on, John. We need to know everything. It's about time we heard the truth."

"It's true. I met her at the bar. I felt responsible for her when she became pregnant with you, Bob." He looked at his son for a reaction. There was none. "I had a place up in Traverse City. A small summer place where I brought her to deliver. I didn't want her reputation to be tainted in Texas. That was her home."

I laughed. "You didn't want her reputation to be tainted. Oh that's choice. A barmaid?"

"She was a gorgeous woman. Long, thick red hair." His eyes misted over. "But I didn't want to get married. I was just starting my career and had a lot to lose. She was a wonderful gal, a lot of fun, just not the marrying kind. So, I moved her up north and we found a good home for our son."

"And you tell us this now because . . .?" I was dumbfounded at the realization that Bob's biological mother was connected to MacGowan.

"Because MacGowan is missing. He's the one I paid to put her in prison."

Bob stood and kicked his chair against the wall. As he stormed from the room, he yelled, "I should have known. Damn you to hell."

Chapter 9

We are always paid for our suspicion
by finding what we suspect.
—*Thoreau*

"Better let him cool down some, John. This must be a doozy of a shock."

"I've been as nervous as a whore in church about telling him. With Blane missing, I was afraid there might be a connection. Otherwise, I don't know. Might have continued to keep it to myself."

"You would have let her stay in prison? She's been there how long now? This is low, John." I wanted to add "even for you" but, for once, held my tongue.

"Don't you want the whole story, Beth? I mean, you know, I had my reasons."

He was pale, and his hands shook as he ran them through his hair. John Gaynor was always a man in control. Now he was smoking and unnerved. "Sure, tell all. But don't leave a single detail out. Not one, hear me?"

"I hear you. Get Bob back in here. And can I have a refill on the cocoa?"

Without a word, I filled his cup and went upstairs to find Bob.

"Guess this explains the cigarette butts, huh?" Bob stood, clenched his fists, and banged them against the wall.

"We need to go downstairs and hear the entire story. Your dad is going to finally tell us the truth. All of it. He promised."

"Yeah. Promises. I've been spoon-fed shit my whole life. I wonder if my folks knew or did John lie to them, too? I trusted him, Beth. I trusted him."

His eyes glistened over. I felt helpless, but knew I had to find the inner strength to figure out this mess.

"John's waiting for us. Let's hear him out."

I guided Bob down the stairs and, as we walked into the kitchen, I said, "John, we'll listen, but we need you to be one hundred percent honest. If you can't or won't do that, you need to leave."

The only sound was the wind's intermittent howling—ominous background music for the scene. John stood. I took a deep breath, bracing for the inevitable.

"No. I'm not leaving. I need to pace. Oh—can I have something stronger than this cocoa?"

I did not want more stalling. "Just talk. Sit, stand, pace, whatever, but no booze."

John, a man used to being in charge, was at a loss for words. "Where do I start?"

Bob glared at John. "Shit. Try the beginning. When you knocked her up."

"Crude, Bob. Please don't think of it that way. We were young. Well, she was young. I was financing a broadcasting network out of San Antonio. I'd already made a killing in real estate, a few good investments and—uh—I gambled some."

"It's getting better. This is a damn soap opera. My God in heaven."

"Bob, please, don't interrupt. Let John talk at his own pace—tell the story the best he can. He's *trying* to be honest here."

"It's okay, Beth. I deserve all that he's got to sling at me. I went to Vegas and hit it. I never gambled, really. Only occasionally. You know. A poker game or two. I put a hundred silver dollars in a machine and got back—well— a lot. I went back to San Antonio and visited this bar to celebrate with some buddies. There she was. I'd never seen anyone so gorgeous. On her break, I slipped her a few hundred bucks. Those gals didn't make much."

"And wait, let me guess, she showed you her thanks?"

"Bob, stop!" I yelled, "No more degrading comments. That was cheap."

"Cheap? You want *cheap?* Check my genetic makeup."

John swirled around. "Now hold it right there. I will *not* have you talk about Robin that way. It wasn't like that at all. Not at all. She was kind and loving. Her job was just that—a job. She was in college and needed to work. You wouldn't understand that, though. Maybe I've made it too damn easy for you."

"Shut up!" I shouted. "It's not the time to make judgments or to place blame. John, please, tell us what happened. My father will be here soon and I *really* don't want him to become a part of this."

I lowered my head.

"None of your saints will help with this one, unless there's a saint for—"

"Bob, actually there is a saint for family harmony. Saint Dymphna. Can't hurt." I prayed. Bob shut up.

"She didn't want the money, but I told her I had plenty. She made me smile and laugh. I was a lot older...."

"Well, Bob, guess that's a trait you inherited." Vic surprised us all with another unannounced and unexpected entrance. She stood behind us in the kitchen doorway, brushing snow from her jacket, B.A.D. under her arm. "Damn dog got out when I opened the, yes, unlocked door. Looks like I made it in time for the fireworks."

"Sit down and shut up," I yelled. "This indirectly affects you. Keep your lips zipped and listen!"

Vic tossed the pup on the couch and, for once, did as told.

John continued. "After awhile, Robin and I got closer. She refused to, well, get intimate without a commitment. So I proposed. She got pregnant straight away. I didn't really want to get married. I'm not proud of that, but it happened. She was crushed. She wanted that baby—you, Bob—but I was in no way ready to be a dad, ya know? So I moved her to Traverse City, away from her friends. She called her family, once she got to Michigan, and told them we were going to get married. Pissed me off, but what could I do? She told them we'd come back in a few months. Couldn't leave for awhile because I had business to tend to up here. They bought the story." John cleared his throat and continued. "I begged her, pleaded with her, bought her tons of jewelry, promised her everything but the damn moon to not abort our baby. She was angry— but she loved me. I'll give her that much. I convinced her to relinquish you—that we would have other babies— once we could be more settled. She finally listened to reason and let you be adopted. I knew a family that wanted a baby, and, there you go."

Bob spoke, his eyes fixed on John. "So you lied to her." His tone was flat and emotionless. "You son of a bitch."

"Son—"

"Don't even presume to call me your son. I accepted my adoption my entire life. I've had a great life. I have a great life now. But this? You lied to her. That's emotional blackmail, John!" Bob stood up and poured a Scotch, pointedly not offering one to John.

I asked, "How does Blane factor into this?"

"It was years later—Bob was already a prominent broadcaster. Robin wanted to open a bar, so I bought her one in Austin. Plenty of money to be made on Sixth Street. She overheard some of the state senators talking and came to me with what she'd heard. Bob, she discovered your wife knew there were plans to kill Glinnis. He'd just been elected."

"Glinnis? He was the lieutenant governor that died in office," Vic groaned. "Jesus, Joseph, and Mary."

Bob smashed his glass against the counter. Scotch spilled onto the white tile. His teeth were clenched—his jawline rigid. "I should kick your ass. You're as bad as those bastards that killed Glinnis."

"I wanted to protect her! She called me and said we had to talk. I hadn't seen Robin in years, but I flew her to Grand Rapids. I explained how I needed to keep a watchful eye on things. This was dangerous business. She agreed to stay here a few months. One night she went downtown, to the Moosehead Tavern, and I called Blane. Told him to get the cops to arrest the redhead for solicitation. We set her up. I had to keep her safe." He took a deep breath, lowered his head, and continued, his voice shaking. "Blane was about to retire and wanted to go out with a splash. He orchestrated a sting, complete with cocaine, and prosecuted the call girls. Gave Robin the max and then some. She was made 'an example.'" Tears fell from his eyes. "God, oh God, I'm so sorry."

Victoria asked, "Why Blane?"

John shrugged his sagging shoulders. "He needed money to keep his folks' whiskey business afloat. His dad had recently died and didn't leave him or his brother anything but the barebones distillery. He was vulnerable."

Bob asked, "Where's Robin?"

"At Robert Scott Correctional. In Plymouth. She's safe. I haven't seen her much."

We let out a collective sigh.

"Now what?" I asked.

"Well, now I'm wondering if someone discovered Blane wasn't the most upfront judge. People have killed for less."

"But who would have a motive?" I asked.

"Parsons," Bob said. "He has to be a part of this. John, you went to see him and so did Blane. What's his part in this shit?"

"Parsons and Blane were school buddies. Maybe even fraternity brothers. Anyhow, they were chums. Sounds like Blane was being visited by nightmares. Maybe even getting a conscience. That's conjecture, of course. I don't know. But I think Parsons was the last one to see MacGowan."

"What makes you say that?" I asked.

"Well, those were my cigarette butts at your place, Vic."

"*What?*" Victoria shrieked.

"Well, Blane's and mine. We were together before he went to see Parsons."

Vic shook her head. "Holy shit."

"Yeah. Once he woke up, he freaked out. He's had this whole trial thing on his mind for years. The demons are singin'. . ."

"So, why did you talk with Parsons?" I wondered aloud.

"I wanted to see what he knew. Blane was going over to talk with him, see if he could do something as the new governor to spring Robin. I wanted to find out if Blane had implicated me at all."

Vic asked, "And?"

"Blane came clean with Jim. He knew Parsons had enough secrets of his own and would keep quiet."

"And?"

"God, Vic, let him talk." I glared at her, raising my voice enough to let her know I meant it.

"So I left and drove around, hoping to spot Blane. I don't buy this vacation shit."

"I don't either," Vic said. "He would have told me. I know he would have. Plus, I called his brother. He didn't know a thing about a vacation. Where the hell is Blane?"

Bob looked from me to Vic to John. "Well, now what?"

"Nothing right now. Daddy's coming over, remember? I want him sheltered from this."

Vic rolled her eyes. "Yeah. Your dad would have a coronary. He's just getting used to you and Bob being together. I don't think we need to go into his parentage."

"So, here's the deal," I said. "Bob and I will stay here until Daddy leaves. To cut the visit with Daddy short, Vic, call us and say you need something. John, visit Robin. Tell her we're going to try and get her out."

"And what am I suppose to do?" Vic asked.

"Go back to Grand Rapids and see if Blane shows up. We need to give him more time. He probably went somewhere to think this through. What he did is a crime. Big time. And John...what *you* did—"

"I know. I paid off a judge. Blane's kept silent all this time. I hope his silence hasn't betrayed him."

I looked around and realized this went deeper than a mere sting operation. Everyone in this room was entrenched in secrets, lies, and fraud. Somehow we needed to right the wrongs . . . if that's even possible. Damn.

CHAPTER 10

Silence is the wit of fools.
—*La Bruyere*

Without a word, Bob escorted Vic and John through the house and opened the front door for them. He took the pup in his arms, took a deep breath, and said, *"¿no es este algo muchacha?* Isn't this somethin', girl?"

Bob, Bowie in tow, walked back to the kitchen. I started a fresh kettle of hot water for another round of cocoa, scrubbed the sink, and sprayed the room with disinfectant until the odor from Bob's spilled Scotch was no longer noticeable.

The doorbell rang, which was odd. We had purposefully left the door unlocked for Daddy. Thinking he'd get the message, we didn't answer the ring. A few seconds passed—the doorbell rang again.

Walking toward the door, I yelled, "Come on in, Daddy, the door's unlocked."

Another ring. I looked through the peephole to be certain it was my dad. There he was. A balloon bouquet covered most of his face, the wind whipping them from side to side.

Opening the door I said, "Daddy! What on earth?"

He walked into the house and laughed. "You thought I'd forget?"

Bob joined me and asked, "What's up, Frank?"

Daddy handed us the dozen helium-filled red, white, and blue balloons. "Go ahead, pop them!"

Knowing Daddy was up to something, I took a ball-point pen from the table next to the door and started popping. Of course, that sent B.A.D. into a barking fit. Jumping and yelping, she went for the ribbons hanging from the balloons.

About halfway through the popping, something fell out from inside a red balloon.

Daddy beamed. "Happy birthday, Texas!"

I read the note attached to a check for $1,845.00. "On this day, December 29th, in the year 1845, Texas was admitted as the 28th state."

"You kids go get something you want for the house."

Bob and I laughed at Daddy's latest trivia. Leave it to him to put smiles on our faces.

"Hey, if it weren't for Texas, I wouldn't have this great son-in-law!"

Bowie had calmed down to wrestling with some ribbon. She began to sneeze and wheeze.

"Oh, my God, Bob, did she get a piece of string or something caught in her nose?"

He pulled the ribbon from her mouth and wiped her nose. "Nope. Probably an allergic reaction. The ribbon is red, after all."

A hearty laugh escaped and Daddy smiled. "You don't really believe she's allergic to things that aren't pink, do you?"

"Nah, but it makes a good story." I took my father's coat and hung it over the nearest chair. "Nice vest!"

Bob and I laughed at Daddy's latest wardrobe addition. To keep in sync with the celebration *du jour*, he wore a Lone Star vest.

"Hope you didn't have that made out of a real flag, Frank. That's illegal, ya know." Bob winked at my father.

"Perish the thought!"

Daddy followed as I walked towards the kitchen. "Want some cocoa?"

"With any luck, you didn't burn the water," Bob said.

I smacked him on the rear for that comment. To anyone who didn't know better, we were just a couple of giddy newlyweds without a care in the world, teasing each other in our new kitchen.

We'd no sooner taken a sip than the phone rang. I picked up and Vic launched into her rehearsed spiel.

"Sure, Vic. Don't worry. We'll be right there. Mind if we bring the pup and stay the night? The weather is only supposed to get worse . . . okay. See ya in an hour or so."

Daddy looked at me. "What's up with Vic? She okay?"

"Her boyfriend left and she's creeped out. You know how she gets. I told her we'd come and stay with her tonight."

"So I heard. That's okay. I didn't mean to stay long. I wanted to surprise you with a little Texas trivia and treasure."

"Thanks again, Frank. Might save it until spring when we work on the yard, how does that sound?"

"Sounds wonderful. While you wait, you'll get some interest on your money. Wise. Too bad I can't stay for the cocoa. My daughter's culinary escapades are always good for a laugh."

Bob chuckled. "That's the truth. Here's one for your special days to celebrate, though. *On this day in history, Christine Elizabeth Pullen did not burn the water for her first batch of hot chocolate.*"

"You two are too much." Daddy's warm smile was exactly what I needed. I kissed him on the cheek, helped him with his jacket, and watched as he drove away.

"Now what?" Bob asked.

"Now we visit your mom."

We changed clothes, packed Bowie's toys and food, and were ready to head to Plymouth when the doorbell rang.

"Wonder what Daddy forgot?"

Coat in hand, I opened the door to find Thorne and Lydia. Holding an extra-large pizza and a six pack of beer, Thorne said, "Almost Happy New Year, kiddo! Long time no see," he laughed. "Where's the hubby? We've come to celebrate!"

"Hey! I thought I got rid of you back at the Log Jam, Thorne. Come on in."

Since Thorne had built the house, he knew his way around and headed, with the food, to the kitchen. Lydia smiled from ear to ear and tossed her knit cap in the air just like Mary Tyler Moore.

I gave her a hug and said, "Hey, good to see you outside the capitol. You're in a better mood than you were earlier."

"Yeah, I'm away from Jerkbutt."

"Now, now, now. That's not an appropriate name for our newly elected governor."

"Appropriate? No. Fitting? Absolutely. That man deserves whatever evil comes his way. What an ass. "

"Lydia, really. He's not all that bad. I think he's really trying to change. He's quit smoking and seems to be less gruff when he speaks."

"Yeah, but he still scratches his back on the door frame. Drives me nuts. I don't think he has the best interests of his constituents in mind. He's driven by one thing and one thing only. Himself. I hate that man. I hate everything about him."

"Oh well, you only have a few more days to deal with him. Count your blessings."

Bob walked in with Thorne carrying paper plates stacked with pizza and chips.

Thorne smiled and said, "We *are* counting our blessings. That's why we're here to celebrate! We're engaged!"

In tandem, Bob and I said, "*What?*"

"We're engaged," Thorne repeated. "You know, we're getting married? 'Til death us do part and all that?"

I threw my arms around Thorne. "Get over here, girl. This is a group hug."

"Bob, would you be my best man?"

"Wow. I never thought you'd—well, you know. I mean Lydia's always …damn." He laughed and shook his best friend's hand. "You bet. When? I mean—wow."

I smiled at Bob. "Tongue-tied, Larken? Never thought I'd see the day. A politician, a broadcaster lost for words. This needs to be another one of Daddy's special days in history."

"Beth, would you be my matron of honor? We're not Catholic, is that still okay?"

"Lydia! Of course it's okay! This is the best news! Tell us everything!"

"Well," Lydia said, "We were hoping we could get married here. By the river this spring. We would have a pastor—but we want it casual. Maybe have the reception at the Log Jam."

Bob smiled. "Now you're talking!"

"I'd like Ken and Kathy from the gift shop to make a bridal registry for me. Think they would?"

"No doubt in my mind," I said. "They'd do anything for you. Oh, my gosh, this is so wonderful!"

Bob hoisted a beer in the air. "To the future Mr. and Mrs. David Hawthorne."

"You'll be able to plan all you want, now that you're not working, Lydia." I love weddings. This news put a much-needed ray of hope in my heart. It's not all doom and gloom.

Lydia cut my silent 'thank you' to Saint Joseph short.

"I asked Parsons if he had a place in his administration for me. The prick said 'no.' I put in eight years as the governor's executive assistant and he tells me no. He had a totally incompetent staff. No one wanted to work for him. He couldn't keep an assistant. I was always covering his ass when he made some stupid comment in public. Now we have him heading the entire state. Stan hated to see him become his successor. Absolutely hated it. I wish there were some way we could recall him before he signs even one bill."

"Man, Lydia, I had no idea you felt so strongly."

"Beth, you have no idea."

"Can we drop this and talk about something happier? Like the honeymoon?" Bob's earlier tears had been replaced with a look of joy.

"Wait!" I strolled over to the piano, the pup trailing not far behind.

I sat and played Wagner's *Bridal Chorus*. "I can record it and play it back using my MIDI rail. Daddy had it installed on the piano before he gave it to me. Listen!" I played a few more stanzas and hit the playback button. "Voila! What do you think?"

The three of them stood and stared.

"Beth," Bob said, "You're amazing. I didn't know you could do that."

"I have many hidden talents, my dear."

"Which brings me back to my earlier thought. What about the honeymoon, Thorne?"

B.A.D. found Lydia's purse on the floor and started to sniff and bark.

"Hush, dog!"

"Remember, she only responds to Espanol. *'Silencio!'*"

She didn't stop. "Do you have a left-over sandwich or something in there?" Bob asked, "She's goin' nuts."

"No. Let me put it on the table."

Bowie jumped on the couch and lunged for the purse, barking and yelping.

"Dump it out," I said. "Let's see what you've got that's so special."

Lydia took out her wallet. Bowie didn't stop. She removed her makeup case and checkbook. Bowie kept barking.

"The only thing left in there is a bag from my trip last weekend." She pulled out a small velvet drawstring bag. Bowie stopped barking and began sniffing the bag.

"Good taste. It's a jewelry pouch from my brother's place in Charlevoix."

"I didn't know you'd gone to see Marty," I said.

" I needed a break from the transition. Dave and I went there looking at rings. Marty designed our rings and I got this as an engagement present."

She placed a copper lapel pin in my hand. It was an open heart with a charm dangling from the top. The charm was shaped like Michigan.

"I figured if Parsons can have a ring shaped like our state, I could have a necklace. Isn't it gorgeous? The copper is from the Upper Peninsula."

Dave put his arm around his fiancée. "Which brings *me* to the honeymoon."

"It's about time these two let you talk," Bob said.

"We've decided to go to Mackinac Island. Where you two met!"

"Can we trust you so near the governor's summer residence?" I asked. "You won't booby-trap it or anything, will you? I really mean it, Parsons has softened some."

Lydia's voice became harsh. "What's *with* you and that man all of a sudden? He's *about* to ruin our state!"

"He offered me a job."

"Holy shit," Thorne exclaimed. "You can't be telling the truth. Bob, please tell me your wife's delusional."

"Nope. I was there. He wants her to work on *positive PR*."

"Now that would be a job and a half!" Lydia sat on the sofa and reached for her pizza. It was gone. Paper plate and all. "Didn't you bring the pizza in?"

"Oh no." Thorne said.

Bowie was under the piano bench sound asleep. The pizza was nowhere to be found.

Thorne looked at the pup. "She's quick and she's quiet. A real stealth dog. We were so worked up over the wedding and Parsons—she saw an opportunity and seized it." Thorne started laughing. Bob started laughing. It was one of those contagious things. Lydia joined the hysteria.

"No wonder she didn't jump on the piano bench with you, honey. She's bloated."

I sighed. "Yeah. At least it's nothing lethal. You have to admit she has good taste. Pizza and jewelry."

Thorne said, "We can go and grab a bite to eat. Maybe see if Kathy and Ken want to join the festivities."

"That would be nice, but we were on our way out when you stopped in with the news."

Looking at the stairs, Lydia said, "Oh, I'm sorry. We were so excited. I see your bags. Where are you headed?"

I beat Bob to the punch. "To Vic's. Just to Vic's. She wants some company. We're going over there to play Scrabble. You know, hang out."

Bob walked over to the stairs and hoisted our suitcase and Bowie's bag.

"The dog has her own travel bag?" Lydia gave the pup a nudge. "You alive?"

Bowie opened her eyes, rolled over, and went back to sleep. Gathering our coats from the hall closet, I scooped up the dog and said, "We'll get together on New Year's Eve, right?"

Lydia said, "Yeah. I'm sitting at my desk 'til midnight to make a point. The inauguration is on the first. That desk is still mine 'til then. We can party at twelve-oh-one."

Thorne shook his head. "You're obsessed."

We walked down the driveway, said our good-byes, and headed opposite directions on Willow Highway.

"To Plymouth?" Bob asked.

"Yep. Time we met your mom."

CHAPTER 11

A good scare is worth more to a man than good advice."
—*Ed Howe*

Taking a Michigan map from the glove box, I searched for the most direct route. "A sorority sister of mine lives in Plymouth. It's really a beautiful town. You think we could visit in a few weeks? They have the International Ice Sculpture Spectacular every January."

"You're kidding me, right? An ice sculpture spectacular? This sounds like something your father invented." Bob reached over and patted Bowie's head. "Your grandpa's a corker, gal." The pup never flinched.

"He did not. It's real. All these famous chefs come to town and sculpt big chunks of ice. Sometimes there're two hundred or so. At night they light up. It's gorgeous."

"They shine lights on ice and they don't melt because . . . ?" He took one hand off the wheel and put it over his mouth. Didn't work. The chuckle escaped.

"Don't laugh. It's true. Every year, well, when I was a little girl, Daddy would take Vic and me to see them. Then we'd stay at this Colonial place. I don't remember the name. It's a historic lodge of some sort. We knew we'd get a nickel for every sculpture."

"A nickel? There's more. I can feel it comin'."

"Right. A nickel because they're shiny like ice. As we got older, the nickels turned to dimes, then quarters. I was holding out for the silver dollars except Vic got interested in boys and our weekend trips kind of ended."

Bob turned the radio to his favorite country-western station. "Hon, you do realize you're babbling, right?"

"I'm nervous. It's not every day I visit a prison."

"I'm sure there must be a saint for this."

"Don't joke about that. It's sacrilege. I mean it."

"Sorry. Geeez."

"Let me look." I opened my purse and extracted my palm-sized *Dictionary of Patron Saints*. "Let's see . . . P. Prisoners. Saint Vincent de Paul. Hmmm. Didn't know that."

"Guess your mom didn't think there'd be a reason to teach her little girl about those sort of folks."

"I suppose not, but she's not *really* a prisoner."

"She's in a Level IV facility. How much more of a prisoner do you want?"

"It's not like she committed a crime, really. She's innocent. Isn't there something we can do?"

"That's what I'm going to find out. This isn't right—not right at all."

I can tell when Bob is upset or relaxed. Either way, his voice takes on a thicker drawl.

"Now don't go and get all pissy. I think she will just love that twang of yours, honey. It'll be nice for her to hear some home-type-typical-twang talk."

"Home-type what?" He let out a laugh that shook the seat. "That's a new one. Did you major in making up words?"

I stuck out my tongue, looked at my watch, then down at the map. "Plymouth is about seventy-five miles from Grand Ledge. That's about a three-hour drive. Maybe four if bad weather kicks in."

"Sure. If we ice skate. Proof positive you didn't get a degree in math." It was wonderful hearing Bob laugh again, even though my lack of numeric ability was the target.

Bob's cell phone rang. "Can you get that, babe? I don't want to talk while I'm driving in snow."

I noticed the readout was John's home number. "Hi, John. I thought you were coming to Plymouth. We're on the road." He began giving me directions. "Wait, okay?"

Bob pulled over to the side of the road and spoke with his father, then handed the phone back to me after he said good-bye. "So why is John at home?" I asked.

"He's not coming. He thinks it's best we do this ourselves. And, truth is, she can only have two visitors. As a Level IV, the visits are non-contact. Beth, I don't think I can do this."

"Sure you can. You can do anything. You're a Texan!" I tried encouraging him, but he started tapping the steering wheel. A nervous habit. It was hard for me to fathom what an enormous revelation he'd been hit with earlier.

"Yeah, I'm a Texan. You bet. Born'n bred, right?"

"C'mon, cowboy, I'll be right there with you every single step."

"Texan? Cowboy? I was born in Michigan, Beth. Didn't you listen to any of that? I was born in Traverse City! Hell, that's not even the southern part of Michigan!"

Maybe if I ignored his comments he'd calm down. "You want me to drive the rest of the way? It can't be much farther. We'll find a place to spend the night and visit fresh in the morning."

"Yeah, our unexpected visitors threw our timing off. There's a motel over there. Exterior doors—we can sneak Bowie in—no problem. You brought plenty of treats and her blanket, right?" Bob asked.

"You bet."

In the morning, we helped ourselves to day-old croissants and stale coffee in the motel lobby. I put a plain donut in my coat pocket for the pup. "The gal at the desk said Beck Road is the next exit on the highway. That's the one we want,"

"Okay. Let's get this over with."

Bob turned off the expressway and continued to Five Mile Road. Before us sat a modern beige fortress encircled by three enormous fences topped with razor-ribbon wire. As we turned onto the road that surrounded the perimeter, I looked up at the gun towers. They loomed above us and held armed staff. The patrol guards were in constant motion, surveying the prison and surrounding acreage. More armed personnel stood in wait. I didn't want to know for what.

As we slowed to announce our arrival, Bowie barked. What is it about uniforms that drives dogs nuts? She didn't stop. I placed my hand over her snout to muzzle her hysteria.

"John also wanted to go over some protocol with me."

"Such as?" My hand remained firmly on the pup's snout. Her growls sounded like a rottweiler gone mad.

"Well, he's filled out all the paperwork.. Said something about a Visitor List Form to identify us as immediate family members."

"So John must have been here recently, Bob. I only became a family member a few weeks ago."

"Shit." If he shook his head much more he'd get whiplash.

"Well, hey, maybe he did it by phone. John has his ways to manipulate the system."

Bob grunted his acknowledgment. "He said Robin had to fill out a form, and we had to fill out a form. We couldn't visit without those, but not to worry."

"That right there should make us worry."

At least that made him smile.

As we approached the guard station, we were met with guns pointing at our car. "What's this all about? They think Bowie's a killer attack dog that will overtake the entire facility?"

"Beth, this is a bigtime prison. Don't joke around."

The guard approached the driver's side of the car. Bob popped open the trunk for inspection and reached in his pocket for his wallet. My purse was on the backseat. As I turned to get it, Bowie jumped out of my arms, catapulted over the gearshift, and lunged for the window. The guard drew her gun.

Bob yelled, "No! *¡parada!* Stop, Bowie! No!"

He grabbed her back legs and pulled her in. She yelped, barked, and yelped some more, wiggling and squirming in her attempt to break free. The officer pulled the Mace from her belt and aimed it at B.A.D. Out of desperation Bob grabbed the pup across her midsection and tossed her over the seat. She hit the rear bench and fell onto the floorboard, whimpering.

I began to climb into the rear to help her when the guard said, "Stop right there, ma'am. We need your identification and to search the vehicle."

"My dog . . ."

The guard repeated, "Your identification, ma'am?"

"It's in the backseat! Look!"

The guard looked into the back and said she'd retrieve my purse from the rear if I would contain the animal.

Bob spoke up. "Ma'am—she can't control the dog unless she gets into the backseat. As you can see, the dog is in some distress. Her purse is in the backseat. If you open the door, the dog . . ."

The burly gal with the Mace and gun glared at me. I was clearly no threat, unless you considered me armed and dangerous with a ten-pound pup.

She looked me over. Looked the dog over. Bowie had gone from barking to growling. The low, guttural growls that scare the crap out of people.

"Okay," she decided. "Climb over and get the I.D. Pass it out the window. Do *not* open the door."

I did as she commanded. I decided to stay in the back and comfort Bowie. She was curled up on the floor, shaking. I tried to console her but she wouldn't budge.

"Sir, your identification?"

Bob tried his pants' pockets, then his jacket. "Damn. Where's my wallet?" He looked in the glove box and in the middle console. No wallet.

"Beth, can you check the floor back there? Maybe my wallet slipped out of my pocket and slipped down there."

I held Bowie who still whimpered as I felt under the seats. No wallet.

"Oh shit. I had my wallet in my jeans. When I changed, I didn't . . ."

"Sir," the guard interrupted—her voice edgy and terse. "You can't be admitted without proper identification."

Bob snapped. "I know! Don't you think I know that? I was almost the damn Gover . . . shit."

"Now what?" I asked.

Ms. No Personality responded, "The lady is cleared to enter the facility, but you, sir, you and the dog will have to leave."

"Beth, you go and see what you can find out from Robin. Tell her I'll come back. I promise. I'll stay with Bowie. I guess you'll need to walk from here. I'm sorry."

I bent down and kissed the top of Bowie's head. I noticed her shaking was becoming more pronounced.

"Bob, she's scared half to death. I can't believe you threw her like that."

"What the hell else was I suppose to do? Let her get Maced? I didn't have a choice. Give me her blanket and pass her back. I'll take care of her. You take care of the business inside."

It wasn't easy getting Bowie off the floorboard. She wiggled and whimpered and continued to shake. I wrapped her in the pink blanket and handed her back to Bob with a small bag of treats and her favorite stuffed toy.

"Once she settles down, she'll take a snooze. She's so scared. She was trying so hard to protect us. What a sweetie," I said. " Do you have anything you want to tell Robin or find out from her?"

"Make sure she's okay and knows I'll get her out of there. Tell her I'll see to it. I'm going to talk with the new governor tomorrow. Tell her that for me."

"I will, honey. I love you." I exited the car and blew him a kiss. Bowie was still in his arms, shivering.

As I walked into the Administration Building of the Robert Scott Correctional Facility, the first thing I noticed was the smell. Antiseptics, bleach, and a certain musty odor—too much cleanser and not enough deodorant, I decided. My heels clicked on the sparkling linoleum. A picture of Governor Stanley Melvin hung in the receiving room. In a few days, that would be replaced with a por-trait of James W. Parsons. I stood and looked at the painting for a moment, letting myself reflect on how we'd been a heartbeat away from the governorship of Texas and an election away from Michigan's dome.

After I submitted to another round of identification processes, a guard escorted me to the non-contact visiting room. The scene was right out of a movie: stark and bare, with only a single chair on one side of a glass wall and two chairs on the visitors' side. A speaker system allowed for communication between the prisoner and the people visiting.

I sat in the cold gray metal chair and waited. Then the heavy steel door opened and I watched in amazement. Even dressed in standard prison garb, Robin was excessively endowed. Good thing all of her human contact is supervised, I thought. With a chest like that she wouldn't stand a chance. Her flowing gray hair swirled as she sashayed across the tiled floor and pulled out her chair. Sitting across from me—in the sequestered visiting room of a prison—was Bob's biological mother.

Weaving and cackling, the half witch-half matriarch yelled at me, her voice booming through the speaker, "Girl! I thought no one would ever come for me. How the hell is that old coot, Gaynor? And damn. My kid coulda been governor. I'll be go ta hell."

I closed my eyes and groaned, "Aw shit. This is going to be a nightmare."

Chapter 12

It's not true that life is one damn thing after another;
It's one damn thing over and over."
—*Edna St. Vincent Millay*

Strange to meet my mother-in-law like this. I couldn't shake her hand. I couldn't put my hand on her shoulder for reassurance. All I said was, "Hi, I'm Beth."

"Honey, I know who you are. I read all about you in the paper. What a wedding. Woulda been a kick in the ass to go to that shindig. Cute priest. In my day, priests were old and shriveled with big ole accents. This guy, man, he'd turn any nun's head. And dang. That Amway Grand! They shore do a mean reception, don't they? I saw all them high falutin' waiters. And that dance floor—polished up like a shiny penny." Robin's laughter bounced off the cinder-block walls. "I'll bet you two lovebirds stayed there for yer honeymoon. In one of them first-class suites. I've read about them rooms. Room service with real silver and china. And those sugar packets with the hotel's picture? Yep. I read all about that place. Real first class. And your old man, Frank. Wow. He's loaded, ain't he?"

This wasn't going the way I anticipated. "Excuse me?"

"No need for prissy-pants manners here. Trust me. Just say what you wanna say. Well, not anything you wanna say. We've got these Gestapo types watchin' us."

I couldn't help but smile. Even locked up, Robin had an aura of playfulness. Bob shared her deep, hearty laugh. It was easy to see how John got caught under her spell.

"And quit starin' at me," she laughed. "If I'da known I was havin' a visitor, I'da gone to the beauty shop."

"You what?" I smiled. Her personality was infectious.

"I'da gone ta get m'hair done. I'm a redhead ya know? This place turned me gray." She winked and laughed again.

"Oh. That's right. I remember hearing you had red hair. Red like the state bird, a robin."

"That's me—Robin redhead. The bird . . . they call robin redbreasts." She took both of her hands and patted her chest and laughed again. "M'boobs bob when I snicker. I think that's prolly why another word for laugh is titter."

We both laughed. Robin had broken the ice.

"So, how d'ya like Plymouth Rock?"

"What?"

"You know, Plymouth Rock? They called Alcatraz *the rock*. Plymouth? Where the Pilgrims landed? Plymouth Rock—where *I* landed? Come on, Beth, work with me here. I haven't had no audience in awhile." Her smiled warmed the cold, stark room.

"I think we'll get along just fine, Robin." I meant it.

"So, where's m'boy? He's one handsome fella. Of course, so's his daddy."

"Bob feels horrible. We were in such a hurry to leave, he left his wallet behind. He had jeans on earlier, with his wallet in the pocket, then he changed into something nicer and . . ."

"Yeah. I remember hearing somewhere you babble." She winked at me. The same wink that unnerves me when delivered by Bob.

I felt my skin flush. "Sorry."

"No need to apologize, girl. But you are cute when you blush. M'son's got good taste."

She gave me the once-over. Meeting your mother-in-law for the first time is nerve-wracking enough. Meeting her behind the glassed wall of a prison is downright frightening.

"He'll come back. He wanted me to tell you that."

"So where is he? Can't John pull some strings? He's good at that."

"He's waiting in the car with our puppy. He parked just outside the main gate. Can't go anywhere. No driver's license."

"Wow. M'stand-up son, the politician, driving without a license. Now *there's* a story."

"He's a wonderful man. You can be proud, Robin."

"I am. I am. John sends me clips now n'then. Gotta hand it to Gaynor. He's never kept me in the dark."

"Yeah," I said. "Real great guy. He locked his son's mother in prison." I was still angry at that revelation.

"Hey. He was tryin' t'protect me, yanno? Not so bad here. Got me a TV, a workout room, all the finer things in life. Food's shitty, though. Think you could get me some good Tex-Mex? I'm kinda homesick for somethin' from Rosa's."

"Rosa's Cantina—outside of Austin?"

"You been t'Rosa's? Damn good margaritas."

"Oh, please. Those margaritas." My turn to laugh. "The first time I went out to dinner with Bob, I got a bit tipsy on Rosa's margaritas."

"I see he inherited one of Gaynor's better qualities. 'Get 'em drunk 'n do 'em.' Am I right?" She covered one breast and slapped her thigh with her free hand.

"No. He was a complete gentleman." I hung my head and grew silent.

"I'm sorry, hon. Did I hit a nerve? It's an ugly habit of mine."

"He was still married. I was working for him in Austin. It was a business dinner. That's all."

"Margaret. Yeah. I was real sorry to hear she died." The playfulness left her voice as her face became solemn.

"I saw the whole thing. It was horrible."

"Back to m'boy. He gonna spring me, or what?"

"I don't think it will be that easy, Robin. We just found out you exist. Someone's missing and John thinks there's foul play involved. You might be safer in here. I don't know why, but John always has his reasons."

"Damn man. I may be an old gal now, an old fool—but I've always loved the man."

I smiled at my newly discovered mother-in-law. "Well, if you're an old fool, he's an even *older* fool."

"Hey, we've got somethin' in common. Crushes on older men! That's gotta count for somethin'!" Her smile returned.

It was impossible not to feel at ease in her presence. "Bob's had a great life, Robin. You did the right thing. His parents loved him. He's had the best of all worlds." My eyes teared up. This must be the shock of a lifetime for Bob.

"Now don't get all mushy on me. Save that crap for when I'm outta here and we can hug 'n cry 'n all that girly shit. I tried to do the right thing. Always have. Look where it got me."

Good thing I was on the other side of a glass partition. The heavy sigh that came from Robin could have blown me back to Grand Ledge. "Well, that's something else Bob got from you. He's tried to do what's right, too. Hasn't always worked out, but he's done okay."

"Okay? You call what he's done okay? Okay like hell, girl. He's kicked ass. My son was the lieutenant governor of Texas and walked out standin' for what's right. That's kickin' some serious Lone Star butt."

"That's one way of putting it." How could I help but laugh?

"Then my boy moved back to Michigan and was gonna be governor. I just know he woulda won. What with his good looks and John's money behind him. But his poor wife died. He did the right thing. He dropped out. He was in mournin', poor kid."

I knew the cameras were on us, we were being recorded and the guard was just a few feet away. I didn't think it was time to set the story straight. I kept my head down.

"Beth?" When I looked up, Robin winked. "Yep, girl. All sorts of eyes 'n ears 'round here. This place is bugged more than tricky Dick's White House."

"Your son's been through a lot, but he's young . . ."

"And gorgeous. Don't forget gorgeous."

"I was getting there but you cut me off!" We exchanged knowing smiles.

"So when's that boy comin' back to meet his mama?" Her eyes widened with the excitement of a child about to get her first two-wheeler.

"We'll go home tonight, get the wallet, and hopefully return tomorrow. How does that sound?"

"Just fine 'n dandy t'me. Not goin' anywhere. See if you can't get permission to bring me some decent food."

The guard walked towards the partition. "You know you can't have non-approved property." The guard's monotone voice was staid. The serious tone led me to think we were dealing with an ax murderer or terrorist.

"Excuse me, could you please explain what approved property is?"

Robin spoke up. "This here's m'daughter-in-law."

The guard didn't smile. Didn't say "pleased to meet you." My bet would be that she wasn't a Cotillion grad. "Approved property must be purchased by prisoners here at the prison store. Prisoners can order things from outside but they must be through approved vendors and sent directly here."

"So I guess I can't bring in a plate of nachos imported from Texas."

My humor fell flat. "That would be correct."

I looked at Robin and rolled my eyes toward the heavens. "So much for flying to Rosa's and having dinner Fed-Ex'd." I pursed my lips to contain the laughter. Robin didn't. She let out a roar accompanied by more thigh slapping.

I started wondering how Daddy would take to this newest family addition. Vic would love her. Thorne, he's such a typical male—he wouldn't be able to look beyond her chest. Won't matter that she's his best friend's mom.

"Hey, you had a big Catholic mass, communion and all for your weddin'. You real religious?"

"I like to think I am, or try to be. Why?"

"Ever read the Good Book?"

"Sure." I hoped a lightning bolt didn't strike me down. I hadn't picked up a Bible for months. I still prayed and knew I had an angel on my shoulders, though. I trusted that gave me extra God points.

"Well, they have Bible studies here at the Rock. I can't go, seein's how I'ma risk. Me. An escape risk. Go figure. Anyhow, they print the studies up so's I can read 'em. Somethin' hit me last week. It really kinda spoke to me."

A prostitute who wasn't a prostitute, busted for possessing cocaine that wasn't hers, locked away and not able to go to Bible study. Yeah. That makes sense to me.

"Can't you have a Bible?"

"Oh sure. I ordered it on the Internet. From one of them approved vendor places. Got me a real purdy white leather one, too. You got yourself a pretty Bible, I'll bet." Her smile had softened to that of a loving mother. Talking about religion reminded me how much I missed Mama. It would be nice to have a mother again.

"I have the Bible Daddy gave me for my First Communion." I hoped lightning wouldn't strike or the floor open up and gobble me. Truth was, I hadn't opened that Bible in months. But I had one and I used to read it. "I pray all the time." Okay, that was the truth.

"Well, last week, the lesson was from Timothy. Or at least the book of Timothy. I'm still tryin' to figure out who Timothy was, but he said some great stuff. Well, maybe Paul said them to Timothy. I don't have that part down yet."

"What was the passage?"

"I memorized it. I Timothy 2:8. 'I will therefore that men pray everywhere, lifting up holy hands, without wrath and doubting.' Ain't that nice? They want us all to get together and pray and stuff without fightin' an' bitchin' 'n stuff. I like that."

"I think that's exactly what it says. I'll pray to Saint Norbert. He's the Patron Saint for peace. When you're released, maybe you'd like to come to Mass with us?"

What was I thinking?

"That'd be swell. I'm notta Catholic so I don't know about them saints. But hey, whatever works. I need some new stuff to wear, though. Don't think Padre Tom would like me showin' up in this." Another one of those Bob-type winks. There was no doubt this was his mom. "I'll put on m'manners, too. I have 'em. I was goin' t'college when Gaynor met me. I was flyin' through the air on a swing, over a bar."

"So we heard." I wanted to get off that subject. The details—I didn't want to know. "I can take you shopping as soon as you get released." Now that will be an experience.

"You really think they'll spring me?"

"I didn't say that—but Bob will do everything he can. He's going to talk to the new governor."

"My boy—he has power, don't he?"

"You could say that, yes. He's the best."

"He gets *that* from his daddy." A sly grin crossed Robin's face.

Our discussion was interrupted by the Gestapo lady. Her walkie-talkie crackled. The guard adjusted her head-set and said, "Got it. Will do."

She approached me. "Ma'am. You're Mrs. Larken, correct?"

"Yes. I'm Mrs. Larken. Is our time up?"

Robin interrupted. "Hey, don't make her go—I ain't had a visitor in months. Count up them minutes and she's enti-tled to a long time."

The guard ignored Robin. "Mrs. Larken, there seems to be a problem at the gate. The guard asks that you come out, please. Your husband needs to speak with you."

"He can't call me on your headset?" I asked.

"No clearance for him, ma'am."

Looking at Robin, I promised, "I'll be back. Bob probably has a message for you. They have all these rules. I'll be back."

Before Robin answered, the guard said, "Not today you won't, ma'am. One visit per day."

I protested. "*You're* the one asking me to leave, otherwise I'd stay longer."

"I'm just relaying the message and explaining the rules. Once you leave you can't return. Policy."

Robin said, "It's okay, sweetie. I'll still be here tomorrow. What's one more day? You bring back that son of mine, y'hear? I'll see if I can't gussy up some before then, now that I know y'all are comin' back."

"It must be something important or Bob wouldn't have them page me like that. I'll bet it's good news! We'll see you tomorrow, okay?"

"It's a date, sweetie pie. You go on now and tend to m'son. Give that boy a kiss from his mama, y'hear?"

"I will—I sure will. Promise."

I wished I could touch her—for reassurance. All I could do was put my hand to the glass. I felt like I was in a movie. They always did that in movies.

Robin gave a final wink and was escorted back out of the room.

I walked back through the Administration Building and braced for the blast of cold as I opened the door. I inched gingerly along the walkway, back the way I'd come, trying not to slip on the ice that had formed.

Leaving the prison grounds, I spotted Peg, my red Ford Mustang, parked alongside the roadway. I opened the passenger door and spotted Bob with Bowie huddled in his arms. The pup was still whimpering.

"What is it, honey?"

"Beth, I let you stay as long as I could, but I think there's something wrong with B.A.D. She hasn't quit shaking. I felt her head, her tummy, her snout, but when I touched her right leg she let out a yelp."

"Let's go. Right now. Oh my God, is her leg broken?"

"I think it might be—or bruised—or whatever happens to dogs. I'm so sorry. I really am. It must have happened when I tossed her in the back. I'm so sorry." His eyes filled with tears.

I went into my take-charge mode. "Get out. We need to change seats. You don't have a license. I need to drive. Plus she looks all comfy in your arms, wrapped up in her blanket. It's okay. It's not like you did it on purpose, Bob, it was an accident."

"I know. We toss her back and forth all the time. She loves it. It's like a game with her."

I repeated, "Honey, it was an accident. She probably just bruised her paw."

"Can that happen with a dog?" Bob asked.

I wasn't sure but answered, "Of course! Here. Take my cell phone. Look under *phonebook* for the name Donna. She's my sorority sister. She lives near here. She can tell us where the closest vet or animal hospital is. Tell her we're on Beck Road."

Bob dialed the phone and I started driving.

Chapter 13

The lowest ebb is the turn of the tide
—*Henry Wadsworth Longfellow*

Bob nestled the phone under his chin while petting B.A.D. "Wing Street! Turn!" He spotted the street sign despite the blinding flurries.

I tried to avoid slipping and sliding on the iced-over roads. Driving a Mustang in the snow is something Daddy hadn't considered when he gave me the car for graduation. I stopped at the corner. "Which way?"

"Donna, east or west on Wing?" He laughed. "Okay, make that right or left—which way?"

He turned his head and said, "Turn left. It's just down the road a piece."

I yelled into the phone, "Thanks, Donna!"

Bob disconnected and said, "A prerequisite for your sorority must have been 'failing navigation and math.'"

I spotted the sign, *24-hr Animal Emergency Services*, and eased into the circular driveway. The yellow brick building was arranged like a normal hospital. There was a separate entrance for emergencies and a parking lot to the side of the main building for patients with appointments.

125

We parked and walked to the emergency entrance.

"Bob, look!"

Above the door was a cross—and to the side was a framed picture of Saint James, the Patron Saint of veterinarians. As we entered, I noticed a Saint Francis of Assisi fountain.

"Leave it to you to find a Catholic animal hospital."

At the registration counter, we filled out the requisite forms, gave them the name and number of our vet in Grand Ledge, and noted Bowie's name and date of birth.

A nurse clad in scrubs decorated with various dog and cat breeds greeted us. "What seems to be the problem with this little one?"

Bob said, "Think her right front leg is hurt."

The nurse patted Bowie on the head and said, "Put her down and let's see how well she can walk."

Bob headed toward the door, knowing she would follow. She did—on three legs, dragging her right paw as she limped.

"No protruding bones. No blood. That's good news!"

Bowie starred at me. "Can I hold her? Look at her eyes. She looks miserable."

"Absolutely. We'll put you in room three. The doctor will be with you in no time. Let me take this little angel for x-rays. Her name is Bowie?"

"That's right, ma'am," Bob answered.

Bowie and the nurse left and I thumbed the display brochures.

"Look at this! They even have a little chapel. And prayer cards."

Bob starred at me.

"Here—the Prayer to Saint Blasé . . . 'obtain a cure for this injured leg if this is agreeable to God. Amen.'"

"They have a prayer card for injured legs? You're kidding, right?"

"No, not injured legs—injured anything. You put in what the affliction is, see?"

I passed the small card to Bob just as the doctor opened the door.

"Mr. and Mrs. Larken? You have the white Schnauzer-Westie mix, right? Bowie?"

We took turns and shook the veterinarian's hand. "Yes," said Bob, "Bowie's our dog, how's her leg?"

"Take a seat," said the vet. From the tone of his voice, I believed this could be serious. I bowed my head.

"Try Saint Roch," Bob said. "He helped us find her in the first place."

"You're both Catholic?" the doctor asked.

I continued praying.

"Yes, we are, " Bob said. We're very impressed with your hospital. Never seen nor heard of a Catholic pet hospital."

"How's our puppy?" I asked.

"We have the x-rays. We got her information off the registration form and called her vet in Grand Ledge. Shots all current. Good!"

"And she has one of those chips in her neck in case she gets lost. One of those I.D. things. Just in case you need to mark that somewhere. There wasn't a place for that on the information sheet," I babbled.

The doctor smiled. "You were wise to bring her in. Seems like that little girl has a closed fracture. Her femur." He pointed to a bone in the back of his leg. "Nothing serious."

"Will you have to operate? Put pins in?" Bob grabbed for my hand and squeezed.

"Oh no. We'll anesthetize her, shave the leg, set the bone, and cast it. You'll need to keep her calm and quiet while she's recuperating, though."

We sighed.

"How long will it take?" I asked.

"Not long at all. We'll do it now. There's coffee in the waiting room if you'd like."

"Waiting room? Can't we come back there? I, I mean we, we don't want her put under without us there. She'll be scared."

The vet answered, "She'll be okay. We'll make sure nothing happens to her."

Bob put his arm around me. "If it's not a problem, we'd rather be there."

"All right. I guess we can allow that. Follow me."

We walked down the antiseptically clean hallway. As the doctor opened the door, I noticed a sign that said *Operating Room*. I gasped, "*Operating*? You didn't tell us about an operation! What's going on?"

Bob turned white and my heart raced.

"We use this room to anesthetize the animals."

I looked at Bob. "Bob?" I said.

"Doctor, then what?"

"Then we shave her leg and Nancy fixes her up with a waterproof cast. She'll be all right. She won't be out long."

"How long is not long?" I asked.

"Hard to tell. She'll wake up groggy, so we'll put her in a cage . . ."

"A what?" I yelled.

"It's a cage—see?" He pointed to a black metal pen in the corner. "It's where the pets stay after any form of anesthesia. For recovery. We monitor their heart and make sure there are no complications."

"Complications?" Bob's eyes teared again. "She'll be okay though, right?"

"It's routine. Pets can have adverse reactions to anesthesia just like humans. Most don't. We've checked Bowie's heart and lungs. They're good and strong."

Bob and I sighed in relief.

"Let's get that little girl of yours and get her fixed up."

He left the room and returned with the nurse and the pup. As Bob and I walked over, her eyes grew large and she squirmed in the nurse's arms.

"Can I hold her for just a minute?" Bob asked.

He took Bowie into his arms and whispered, "You're gonna be just fine, girl. *Estoy apesadumbrado, yo realmente.* I'm sorry, really I am." He kissed the top of her fluffy white head and handed her to the nurse.

They put the pup on the table and gave her an injection. Moments later, her eyes closed.

Neither Bob nor I could stand to watch the doctor as he set the broken bone. We heard the razor and turned to find Bowie, still asleep, unaware that she'd been worked on.

The nurse went to the sink and began preparing white goo. She returned to Bowie and wrapped her broken leg with something that looked like heavy gauze.

"What are you doing now?" I asked.

"Putting her cast on."

"No!" I commanded. "Not a *white* cast. It has to be pink! She'll sneeze and wheeze constantly if you put something white on her."

The doctor and nurse stared at me.

Bob explained, his voice shaking with tension. "Now I know this sounds silly, but Bowie doesn't like to wear anything but pink. Just trust us, okay?" For a man who was a broadcaster and politician, he sure turned to mush when it involved his dog.

Without questioning, the nurse transformed the white mixture to pink and casted Bowie's leg.

"Are you finished? Can we hold her now? I want to be holding her when she wakes up."

"We need to keep a close eye on her, ma'am." the doctor replied.

"Beth," Bob said, "why don't I stay in here? I'll get a chair and hold Bowie. You go get some coffee and make some calls. Let folks know where we are. I think I need to be the one holding her when she wakes up."

"Okay," I said. "I could use some coffee. I'll go to the car, turn on the heat, and make the calls."

I stroked the top of Bowie's head, kissed Bob on the cheek, and thanked the doctor and nurse. Then I grabbed a cup of coffee and went out to the car. First I dialed Daddy and explained what had happened. I failed to mention visiting Bob's biological mother in prison—simply said we took a drive to Plymouth to visit Donna. Cutting the conversation short, I phoned Vic—who still hadn't heard from Blane. Final call—John. I told him about the forgotten wallet, about my visit to see Robin, and about the pup's fractured leg. John mentioned stopping by at some point, but I didn't pay attention when he said when that would be. My mind was occupied with thoughts of tending to a pup with a cast.

Several cups of coffee later, Bob, Bowie, and I were back in the car. "We need to go home. I promised Robin you'd go see her tomorrow. And at some point I need to touch base with Parsons," I said.

"Yeah, you promised him an answer about that job."

"He'll have to wait for now. Family emergency." I kissed the pup on the top of her head as she snored in Bob's arms. Maneuvering the slick roads, I found my way to the expressway and headed for home.

My cell phone rang. Bob's hands were full, so I pulled to the side of the road. With all that had been going on, I didn't want to miss any late-breaking news.

It was Victoria checking to see how the pup was. I listened to her worries about B.A.D. That didn't take long.

Then Vic said she still hadn't heard from Blane and didn't want to spend New Year's Eve alone. Since nothing major had transpired on her end, I told her we were all fine and I'd call her in the morning.

"Nothing new, I take it?"

"Nope. No Blane. That doesn't seem to bother Vic as much as the thought of not having a date for New Year's. Oh, and she also wished B.A.D. a speedy recovery."

"Did you call John? Did you tell him you visited Robin? I've been so caught up with Bowie's leg that I didn't even ask. How was it? How is she?"

"It was interesting. She's fine, all things considered. She's colorful, I'll give her that much." I smiled.

"Colorful?"

"Uh, yeah. She's outgoing. No, more like out there." I laughed, remembering her witty comments and boisterous chuckle. "You two have the same wink! That was wild. I should warn you—she's a bit on the, well, the *rough* side. I'm not so sure she ever read Miss Manners' column."

"You two didn't get along? She's crass?"

"No! That's not it at all. I can see how John could be attracted to her. She's quite, um, well, quite curvy. Gorgeous smile. But she wouldn't have made a suitable *wife* for John. That's all I'm saying."

"OOOooh." Bob said.

"I don't think Robin is the kind of woman a man could tame, honey."

"Did you tell her I'd come see her? Explain about the wallet?"

"I did. She's a very selfless woman, Bob. Admirable. I was shocked at first. She's so loud. I guess if the shrew could be tamed, so can Robin." I glanced his way and smiled.

Bob squinted. "I have a few questions for John about this. Something stinks. Why is she still in prison? The sentence, I know, was not only for prostitution but possession. Can't she get paroled? There are ways. Plus, you and I know she didn't do anything wrong."

"You and I know that. John knows that. Blane knows that. I guess Victoria does now, too. But that's all. It's been kept silent, remember? For her protection?"

"What is John protecting her from now, though? I'm no longer a public figure."

We sat there, in silence, and thought.

"This has to tie into Blane, Bob. If Robin can prove she was set up, then she can finger Blane, the evil judge."

"But if Blane is dead—Blane is the only one that can tie John into this. Holy shit."

Despite the condition of the roads, I accelerated. For a variety of reasons, we needed to get home.

Driving up to the house, we saw that the road leading to our house had recently been plowed and our driveway was newly shoveled.

"Looks like Thorne's handiwork," Bob said. "The wind was nasty today. Blew the garbage cans to the ground."

"Glad today was trash day. If they would've been full—what a mess!"

As I opened the car door, I saw a few pieces of trash the garbage men missed. I walked over, stooped to pick them up and noticed a tiny zippered makeup bag behind a small drift of snow next to the curb. It was one of those pouches that come with the buy-one, get-one free cosmetic campaigns. I have a few just like it under my sink.

"Hey, Bob! Are you throwing away my stuff?" I yelled across the driveway.

Bob with Bowie asleep in his arms, pink-casted leg hanging down, joined me by the curb. "Nope. What is it?"

I unzipped the pouch. "Oh, there's just a little lipstick brush in here. And a small sample of lip gloss." Reaching for the gloss container, I saw it was empty. "I'll bet Lydia threw it away when Thorne was plowing. She gets these by the dozens like I do."

"She's more sensible, though, and throws the duplicates away," he said. " Come on—let's go and make some calls."

Bob called Thorne and thanked him for tending to the driveway. I asked if the brush was Lydia's. It was. She'd purchased some perfume on their trip to see her brother and got the freebie. She asked me to throw it away. That explained that.

"I think I'll keep that lipstick brush, honey. I could use it for gloss. The one I have now I can use for lipstick. And those little makeup bags are so cute! I can put some dog bones in them and keep it in my car."

"Oh right. Perish the thought we should pitch adorable bag number three hundred and five." A smile crossed his face.

I looked over. Bob had set Bowie down gently on her pink cushion, and was now struggling to pull a plastic baggie over her cast.

"The vet said to keep the cast dry for the first twenty-four hours. It's one of those waterproof deals, but it needs to harden overnight," Bob said.

"So you're making her a baggie boot? How clever. We should lock the doggie door and take her out on a leash until she's healed. If she tries to chase a squirrel, we're in big trouble. She's supposed to stay calm, after all."

"Well, she's still groggy from the anesthesia so we're in luck for awhile. I think this plastic's on okay. I'm going to find my wallet and make sure I have what I need for tomorrow. Want me to start a fire?"

"Great idea! I'll carry the pup into the kitchen. She can rest while I fix something for dinner. It's been quite a day."

"By the time you burn something for dinner, and I run out and get take-out, it'll be classified a midnight snack."

"Yeah. You look underfed, Larken." My sardonic tone brought a smile to his face. Bob stands six-foot-four and possesses the shoulders of a former athlete. He doesn't work out—doesn't watch what he eats. I swear he stays in shape by just breathing.

"So what culinary delight are you whipping up for your adoring husband?"

"Tomato soup and grilled cheese."

"Can't do much to ruin that. I love burnt cheese and scorched soup." He winked. "It's a deal," he said and went upstairs.

I admit I'm no Betty Crocker. One of the first meals I prepared for Bob was Chicken Cordon Bleu. I liked saying that name, and figured all I needed was chicken with bleu cheese dressing for the sauce. Wasn't sure what the *cordon* was but thought it meant chicken with bleu cheese. The bleu cheese dressing burnt on the pan, but I salvaged parts of the marinated chicken. One bite and Bob spit a chunk of chicken onto his plate saying he was allergic to bleu cheese. I told him he wasn't allergic to bleu cheese—he was allergic to *Roquefort*. How was I to know they're the same thing?

CHAPTER 14

We learn from experience that
we never learn from experience.
—*Bernard Shaw*

I opened a can of soup and went to the refrigerator for the rest of the meal's ingredients. I stirred some milk from the fridge into the pan and turned it on low. Bowie stirred and looked toward the doggie door.

"You need to go potty?" I asked.

She continued to stare at the door.

"I suppose you do, girl. *Out?*"

With that final word—out—she lifted gingerly from the blanket and hobbled to the door. She's finally learned an English word! She was unsteady—her balance off. She clunked her way around the table knocking over the umbrella stand, and barely missed another injury when the pink plastered leg toppled a potted plant.

I threw on a jacket, shoved the mess to the side, leashed B.A.D., and out we went. I heard the crunching sound of tires on snow as headlights turned into the drive. Bowie began frantically barking, but the weight of her cast made jumping impossible. The upstairs deck door creaked and Bob looked out to investigate the commotion.

"It's John. He can join us for our midnight snack."

"It's not midnight."

"It will be by the time we eat. You used spoiled milk. I'll go get Chinese." He shook his head and went inside.

Bowie did her business, and we approached John's car. He jumped out of the driver's seat, as spry as a man much younger. Well into his seventies, John was six foot tall and sported a full head of gray hair. Day or night, he always looked like he was going to a business meeting.

"Hey, John. Come on in. We haven't been home long."

"Oh, the poor pup," he tapped on the cast. "Pink. Figures. You okay, girl?"

John wasn't an animal lover but succumbed to her sorrowful eyes and gentle whimper. "She was bound to get hurt sooner or later with all she gets into."

Bob joined us. "Wasn't her fault this time. It was an accident. Hey, you hungry? I'm going for Chinese."

"Sounds good. And don't forget the fortune cookies. Might help us find MacGowan."

"Guys, let's go inside for a few minutes before you get dinner."

I carried Bowie and settled on the couch. "Bob and I were talking about Blane on the way back from Plymouth. Who knows you bought MacGowan?" I asked.

I looked at Bob. He looked at John.

"Me, Blane, Robin. That was it. Then I told you two and Vic heard it, too. That's it."

"I thought Robin knew—but I wasn't sure. How did she find out? What's going on here?" I asked.

John fixed his eyes on Bob. "Robin's no dummy. She's cagey. Once I told her she was in danger and I'd take care of it—I'd protect her—well, of course, she figured it out."

"Are you sure?" I wasn't about to let up.

"No," John said. "I'm not *sure*. I'm not sure *any* of us are safe."

"Oh great. I feel better now."

"Could Blane have told anyone?" Bob asked.

"That's what I wanted to find out from Parsons, but I couldn't come right out and ask. So I pretended I might give his ideas some financial backing, you know? Depending on whether or not they met with my approval."

"John. Don't tell me. You suggested he hire Beth," Bob said.

"I might have mentioned Beth—but you, Bob. Hiring you was entirely Parsons' idea."

"Go on." I said. My bubble was burst. So much for being in the governor's administration on my own merits.

"So we discussed his stand on the issues you believe in—adoption, education, bilingual issues—commutation and pardons."

"I have a stance on commutations and pardons?" Bob asked.

John said, "Well, I had to see how Parsons felt, in case you got some cock 'n bull idea of asking him to do something for Robin."

"Now with Margaret dead, what could harm Robin?" I asked.

"Herself," John replied.

Bob asked, "Are you saying she's suicidal?"

"No. You met her, Beth. She's a loose cannon."

"You don't think she'd divulge everything, do you? You do, don't you?" I laid Bowie on the floor, by my feet, and placed my head between my hands. I felt a double-dose Excedrin headache starting.

"Don't put words in my mouth."

"I disagree. I spoke with her. She's doing Bible studies and is proud of her son. She even said nice things about you, John."

"Happy to hear that. But I'm not willing to take that sort of risk."

"Has she had many visitors? Who's on her approved list? Does she have any contact with the outside?" Bob asked.

"Where are you headed with this?" I asked.

"Just wondering. If she knew Blane sent her to prison on a bogus charge—or at least a charge that was paid for . . ."

"Honey, no! You can't think she's involved with Blane's disappearance."

"Excuse me, you two, Blane's *alleged* disappearance," John said.

"Right," I groaned. "Alleged. He's nowhere to be found. Hasn't checked in with anyone and is about to break Vic's heart if he doesn't get back here for New Year's Eve."

"Well, then, who else would want to shut Blane up?" I asked.

"No clue," John said. "Bob, you'd better go for that Chinese before they close."

"Let's all go. Forget take-out." I said.

"What about Bowie? Someone needs to stay with her," Bob said.

"We'll take her bed with us. I'm sure they won't mind at Chu Lin's."

"Beth, the Health Department. We can't take her in a restaurant."

I smiled. "Just like I told Robin, you always try to do the right thing. Lin will let me put her upstairs in her apartment. I've done it before. We'll only be an hour or so and it's late."

"All right then. She's packed from the trip to Plymouth," Bob said.

I leashed Bowie and decided to let her walk to the truck. That way she could do her business. As we approached the truck she barked, her nose in the air, pointing to the curb. "What's wrong, girl?" I asked.

She kept barking and pulled on her leash. Poor thing. She was lopsided—all ten pounds of fluff leaned left to favor the broken leg.

"Okay, let's go take a look."

I called to Bob, "Get the truck warmed up, honey. We'll be right there. John, why don't you go ahead? We'll meet you at the restaurant."

We made it a few feet when Bowie stopped and peed.

"Good girl! There was nothing wrong, you just needed to go!"

She started pawing at a small bump in the snow. Digging single-pawed didn't work, though, so she lowered her little snout and rooted. She lifted her head and a portion of a plastic bag dangled from one side of her mouth.

"You little trash monster. *Now* what did you find?" I removed the piece of opaque plastic. The bag had torn during her scavenger hunt. I pushed the snow aside with my boot and saw the remnants of a pharmacy bag.

"What's this, girl?" I looked inside. An empty cigarette patch box.

We walked back to the truck. "John needs to put his trash in the garbage can. Look here." I showed Bob the empty box of patches.

"Remember? There was some trash missed by the garbage men. Must have been part of that. Wait. I don't think those are John's, Beth. He smokes now and then. You're not suppose to smoke and wear those things."

"Well, then, whose could they be?" I asked.

"We'll ask him at dinner."

We arrived at Chu Lin's just as they were locking the door, but Mr. Chu let us in when he recognized us. Bob joined John at the table and I got Bowie nestled upstairs with the owner's daughter, Lin. As I walked towards the table, I stopped and smiled. Bob and John were looking over the menu and laughing . Guffawing, practically.

"What's so funny, guys?"

"Bob asked me what those good pork dumplings were called and I said dim *wit*—I meant dim *sum*. He thought I was calling him a dimwit." They looked at each other and laughed even louder.

"You two," I shook my head. "Bowie's all snug. She'll be fine. I told Lin not to feed her anything. She can't eat until the morning because of the anesthesia. I read that in the little brochure. Then it's probably better if we make her rice or scramble some eggs," I babbled.

"I doubt that." Bob said.

"Doubt what?" I asked.

"I doubt it would be better for her to have rice or scrambled eggs. If the broken leg isn't bad enough, you'd torture her with your cooking?" He ducked behind the open menu.

"Good thing I love you so much, or I'd stab you with this chop stick." I stuck my tongue out and crinkled up my nose.

"I can't believe it's ten o'clock. This has been one helluva day," Bob said. "I plan to sleep 'til noon tomorrow."

"You two aren't going to Lansing to bid a fond farewell to Stan?" John asked. "It's his last day as our governor. He and Lydia are staying put until the very last moment."

"So I've heard. I really should give Parsons an answer." I tapped my spoon on the table. "Don't know—now that I know you persuaded him to . . ."

"Wait a second, Beth," John said. His voice became louder and he leaned on his elbows. "I just mentioned your name. Threw out some other names, too. I think you'd do a fabulous job."

"Thanks," I said.

Bob added, "It also wouldn't hurt to have you keep tabs on what's going on."

I threw my napkin at him. "You're bad!"

He smirked. "You know what Thorne told me. No lie. Lydia told him. Parsons put that plastic stuff—you know, that you put under computer chairs—he put that over the entire carpet in his office!"

"The entire office? You're joking, right?" I still have trouble knowing when Bob is serious or telling a Texas tall tale.

"No joke. All except for a small area by the door. I know you're dying to know why." His eyebrows did their little up-and-down routine. All he needed was a cigar to complete the Groucho Marx look.

"Oh, do tell. John, you ready for this?"

He cleared his throat. "My bullshit detector is sounding a warning."

Our soup arrived. Bob waited for the waitress to leave, then said, "He had plastic matting put down so he would-n't have to get up to get soda and cookies from the other side of the office."

"Excuse me?" I asked. I know I have auburn hair, but I was having a blonde moment. This did not make sense.

"He won't have to get off his ass. He can just scoot his desk chair over to the credenza and help himself to Pepsi and cookies whenever he wants. Isn't that a stroke of genius?"

Unfortunately, I'd just sipped some soup. It went flying.

"Sorry," Bob said. "Just thought you'd like the inside scoop."

"Always nice to have insider's knowledge," John said.

I smiled at John, and nodded my head. "You'd be the one to know."

We polished off our entrees in record time. Stress always makes me ravenous.

"Will you be able to stop by tomorrow night, John? We'll start the party around nine. Then Bob and I thought we could caravan over to the capitol to usher in the new year with Stan, Bitsy, and Lydia."

John sat for a moment, then said, "Sounds like a plan. The State of Michigan will be losing not only a first-rate governor, but a fantastic first lady. Bitsy is one of those 'women behind the man' you read about. She has it all. Like you, Beth. You would have made a beautiful first lady."

I was flattered. "Thank you, John. I agree, Bitsy is a jewel. I can't believe, when I first met her, I thought she was part of the staff." The memory of that night—the night I met Bob—warmed my heart. One of those times a girl never forgets. "But Shelly Parsons will be a terrific first lady. She's charming, intelligent, and filled with love. She told me she's making public libraries her primary focus."

John nodded his head, "She's a good woman. I feel for her. She's standing strong with her husband, though."

We finished dinner and John opened his fortune cookie. It read, *Something missing will be found.* "Interesting," he said.

"I don't believe in those things, it's like a psychic. Bad stuff," I said. Bob started to crack open his cookie and I flashed him the evil eye.

"Fine then," he said, and left it on the table, next to mine.

I retrieved a sleeping Bowie and we said our goodnights at the restaurant door.

"So, John, our place tomorrow—New Year's Eve—nine o'clock?" I asked.

John rubbed Bowie under her chin. "Sure thing. Hopefully, Blane will be joining us, but I doubt it."

"Oh—John," I asked, "I just remembered I wanted to ask you something. Do you know what kind of smoker's patch Parsons uses? Did he ever mention them to you?"

"Can't say as he did, no."

He turned his attention back to Bob. "Aren't you driving down to see Robin in the morning, son?"

Bob smirked. "That I am. It's about time I find out where my charm and good looks come from."

"No need to drive to Plymouth—you got it all from me," John said.

Bob smiled. "Spoken like a true father."

John smacked Bob on the back, the way fathers do. "Great night, isn't it?"

I looked at the winter sky. Only one night left in this year—the year I met and fell in love with Bob. The moon glistened amid a palette of cotton-like clouds. My daydreaming was cut short by the ringing of John's cell phone.

He looked at the readout. "Hot damn! It's MacGowan!"

He answered the phone, then looked up at us with an indescribable expression. We both stared back.

"The line went dead."

Chapter 15

Everyone is a moon and has a dark side
which he never shows to anybody.
—*Mark Twain*

John pressed the redial button on his phone. He looked at us and said, "Voicemail." He tried again. This time he left a message. His voice had a bit of an edge as he said, "MacGowan, it's Gaynor. Where the hell are you? You know the number—call it." He shoved his phone in the holder attached to the belt beneath his jacket. "He's probably in one of those spots with poor reception. Happens to me all the time. Wish they'd perfect these things." He shook his head. "Damned service providers. You'd think they'd get it right for all they charge."

I nodded. Best not to disagree with John when he's frustrated. "At least we know he's all right," I said.

Bob took Bowie from me and I stretched from side to side. Amazing how a limp dog with a bum leg can feel like a ton in your arms.

Adjusting the ten pounds of dead weight, Bob said, "He's probably trying everyone. Seeing who he can get through to. I'll bet he tried Vic, but she gets even worse reception than out here. It's that apartment of hers. All those trees, you know?"

I shifted my eyes from John to Bob. "I'm calling Vic to let her know we heard from him."

"Can it wait until we get home? It's freezing out here."

"Good point. John. If Blane gets through to you, let us know right away, okay?"

John answered, "I'll let you know, but it's late. I'll call you in the morning, either way."

We said our good-byes—each car turning its separate way.

Bob took the twists and turns in the truck with ease. "Man, John's edgy. He got all huffy when Blane didn't answer."

"Yeah. When things don't go his way, it's not a pretty sight."

The truck's heater hadn't fully kicked in and Bob exhaled a puff of frosty air.

"That man better get back here before tomorrow night or he'll have hell to pay when he does."

"No joke. Blane can't miss this party," I sighed.

Bob gave me a sympathetic look. "I know. Vic will make life miserable if she doesn't have a man to kiss at the stroke of midnight."

"Oh, it's more than that. It's such a special night. I want everything to be perfect—it's our first New Year's Eve together!"

"Women always remember firsts," he smiled. "It's a hormonally based predisposition."

"I love it when you use those fancy words." I wanted to lighten the mood some. "Speaking of fancy words, I heard something on the radio and forgot to ask you about it." I tried to keep a straight face. "Do you know what the plural of spouse is?" Before he could answer, I said, "*Spice!* The plural of *spouse* is *spice*." I attempted to maintain the charade, but my lips quivered with the beginning of laughter. "Get it? Two spouses equals spice?" I burst out laughing. Sometimes my own jokes break me apart.

"Oh brother," Bob moaned. "Are you sure you didn't sneak in a few drinks with dinner?"

"No way! I learned my lesson at Rosa's. Drinks—me—you. Lethal combination."

Bob raised his eyebrows. "Sounds okay by me! But who in their right mind would want two wives?"

I shot him the evil eye. "Oh, like two women at once never happens in politics. Yeah, right."

"You said plural of *spouse*, Beth. That's entirely different."

"Pardon me, kind sir." I stuck my tongue out for effect.

Our banter awoke Bowie, who yawned and attempted to stretch her legs. Her head flinched and all ten pounds shook. I tried to adjust her body to accommodate the leg that was sticking out.

"Poor thing," I said. "This will take some getting used to."

"Yeah. For all of us. I'll have to remember to carry her up and down the stairs. Not sure she should be attempting that on her own. And we'll need to keep her leashed when she goes outside. If she tries to chase a squirrel, or a raccoon comes after her . . ."

"Oh, stop that! It's not funny. Tease all you want—I'm keeping the doggie door bolted."

At home, we settled in and I checked the answer machine for messages. There were two.

"This is your new Governor. Beth—Mrs. Larken—would you please stop by my office in the Olds Building tomorrow so we can discuss your possible position with my administration. Call Lydia. Tomorrow's her last day. It'll make her feel important. I'll be here all day."

Click. I hit erase and went on to the remaining message.

"Bob, it's Stan. I got your call. I will be signing pardons and commutations tomorrow—my final act as Governor. What's up? Call anytime."

Click.

"Bob? You called Stan?"

"Yeah, when I went upstairs to change. When you took Bowie out—before John showed up."

He scooped Bowie into his arms and I followed them upstairs. He placed her in her quilted pink doggie bed. This is one spoiled dog. We brushed our teeth and climbed into bed.

Bob pulled me to him and said, "I called Stan to see if I couldn't talk to him about Robin. He wasn't in, so I left a message. Man, I would hate to think we'd need to ask a favor of Parsons. Plus, just going into office, I doubt he'd sign any commutations or pardons, you know?"

"True. Good thinking. Which would Robin get, a commutation or a pardon? Not sure if I understand the difference." All these legal terms make me shudder.

"Pretty straightforward. A commutation is when they reduce the sentence to what you've already served and you're put on parole. A pardon—the prisoner's sentence is voided and the prisoner is freed."

My eyes widened. "Poof—free. Just like that?"

"No, not exactly." He rolled on his side, propped up on one elbow, and squinted his eyes. "It's pretty detailed, but it looks like there is a way around the system."

"Isn't there always?" I asked. "How does it work? How can she just be freed like that?"

"Ah, the power of a governor." He sat upright. Talking about power always energized his voice.

"It would be great if Robin could get a pardon!" I was excited to think she would be able to leave the Rock and we'd get to know her better. Okay, I was excited but nervous as hell. She wasn't exactly June Cleaver. We might have to ease her into the family.

"Whatcha thinkin' about, babe?" Bob asked.

"Oh, I was thinking how it would feel to have some sort of mother again."

"Some sort? That's a funny way of putting it," he laughed.

"Well, Robin isn't exactly like my mama."

"I gathered as much. Tell me more about her. Am I like her at all?"

"Yeah." I said, a grin threatening to take over my face. "You're both old."

Bob grabbed me and stuck his tongue in my ear. "Knock it off. I'm serious. Tell me about her."

I pushed him away, laughing, and rubbed my ear. I wasn't sure how to describe Robin. "You need to meet her to see the similarities. She winks like you. She's definitely an extrovert. Between John and her it's easy to see how you'd be at ease in public." That was no lie. "Her voice is a bit loud. Wouldn't hurt to get her a voice coach." I smiled so he wouldn't think I was being critical.

"Like they use when training broadcasters?" he asked.

"Exactly! She could use some work with grammar . . ."

"Oh man. You're not painting a pretty picture here, girl."

"Oh no! She's charming and witty. If she wore one of those minimizer bras, she could . . ." I laughed. The combination of talking and laughing made me choke. I sat up and Bob smacked me on the back. I coughed. "Thanks. Sorry about that."

"C'mon. Be serious. This is no joke," he said.

"I'm *trying* to be serious. I just keep getting visuals of your mom showing up for a fundraising event in a tight V-neck top. She's colorful. I'm not sure what else to say."

Bob looked forlorn.

"Hey, I'm sorry. I wasn't being critical. She's terrific. Really. She just isn't what I expected. That's all. It's not a negative thing." I tried to convince myself, but I know how the media works. They'd jump all over this if she got pardoned and the truth came out."

"You think she should come live with us?" Bob asked.

"She could stay in the guest house, I suppose." The guest house wasn't really a guest house. Thorne had converted the barn into a small retreat, complete with a full bathroom. It's where I did my writing. "We could get a microwave and little refrigerator."

"You know there's more problems tied to this than I imagined at first. We need to think this through." Bob slumped down on his pillow, folded his arms across his chest, and closed his eyes.

"You want a massage, hon?" I asked. He remained silent. "You okay, Bob?"

"I suppose. John had her incarcerated for a reason. She overheard threats and was discovered. If she's let out of the Rock, she's in danger. The way to get to John is through me or my mom. No one knows she's my mom." His kept his eyes closed and started rubbing his temples.

"They don't know—yet. But she talked about you in the visitation room. Mentioned you as her son. The folks at those prisons . . ."

"I know. More loose cannons. Damn, Beth, what do I do?"

"You call Stan. You see if you can get Robin out of that place. We'll worry about the rest later. Until you talk to Stan, we don't know if her freedom's possible."

I took the phone from the nightstand next to me and handed it to Bob. "Here. Make the call. He stays up well past midnight. I'm sure tonight is no exception."

It wasn't.

"Stan—it's Bob. Yeah. I need to talk to you as soon as I can in the morning. I have one last favor to ask of Michigan's great Governor before he leaves office. Have you got a hearing set tomorrow for any last commutations and pardons?"

There was a pause.

"Think you could swing one more? Uh-huh. I know— isn't there some way we can expedite a clemency application and Parole Board review? Okay. Sure. I understand. I'll be there at six. Thanks, Stan." He handed the phone back to me.

"Six? Six in the morning?" I *hate* mornings. "And aren't you going to Plymouth to see Robin?"

"Yes, to both. Hopefully, when I see Robin, I'll have some good news! Don't worry, I'll let you and the pup sleep in. You need to get ready for the party, anyhow."

"No way! I'm going! If he signs a pardon for your mom, you think I want to miss *that?*"

"Okay. I'll wake you up. I'm warning you, though. It could take awhile—maybe a few hours—at the capitol."

"No problem. I'll talk to Parsons while you're with Stan. Bowie can come with me. If Parsons gets gnarly, I'll sic her and her killer cast on him. Our own personal Terrier Terrorizer." We both laughed. "This political stuff is nuts— and I want to get involved with this again? I must be crazy."

"You are, but I love you in spite of it." Bob kissed me on the nose.

"I'm going to try Vic. Tell her we'll be on the road early."

"I know. You two always check in. That's good. Make it short, though. Six will be here before you know it and you'll be grumpy enough as it is."

I dialed Vic. "It's busy! She must be talking with him now." I looked toward the heavens and smiled. "Oh thank you, Saint Raphael, thank you."

"And Saint Raphael is . . .?"

"The saint for lovers."

"I thought that was Saint Valentine?"

"That's the saint for the greeting card industry."

Bob laughed. "You're too much. I love you, you nut." He curled up next to me—I nuzzled under his chin—and we kissed goodnight.

"I love you too, honey." I whispered.

The phone rang. I looked at the clock and slammed a pillow over my face. Bob reached over my fetal-positioned body and nudged me.

"Beth! The readout says it's Vic. Answer the phone."

"What?" I groaned.

"Shit. Hello?" he said. "Just a minute—hold on."

"Beth. Beth! Here." He handed me the phone. "Vic's wired. Deal with it." He got up, walked into the bathroom, and shut the door.

I sat up, half-asleep, and looked again at the clock. "Vic, are you alright? It's four in the morning."

I listened to her litany of excuses, ranging from

Pookie's furballs to her manicure with claw imprints. "Apparently, the kitty's keeping you awake?" I held the phone away from my ear. Vic's voice thundered through the line. B.A.D's eyes opened and she yawned.

Getting a word in between her rants wasn't easy. "I tried to call you last night but your line was busy. Were you talking to Blane?"

That's when the sobbing started. She wailed so hard the words caught in her throat as she tried to speak.

"Calm down, Vic . . . slow down . . . breathe. It wasn't Blane?"

Bob returned to bed, stared, and shook his head. I covered the mouthpiece and explained as Victoria sobbed into the phone. "I think she's having an anxiety attack. It wasn't Blane on the phone last night. Pookie, you know, the kitty Blane gave her for Christmas? Pookie knocked the phone off the hook in the bedroom. Vic fell asleep in the living room with the TV on so she didn't hear that annoying beep—you know—the one that tells you to put the receiver back?"

More husbandly head nodding. He's had practice.

I turned my attention back to the phone conversation. "Vic, listen. Blane's fine. He called John last night. He probably tried to call you, too. Get off the phone and make sure you put it somewhere Pookie can't reach."

I stared at a silent phone.

"Bob, she said 'oh my God he might be trying to call right now' and hung up. Just like that. No thank you. No see you later tonight. Nothing."

Chapter 16

A wise man hears one word and understands two.
—*Jewish proverb*

Now I was awake. Irritated and awake. "I'll put on a pot of coffee." I needed to focus on the day ahead and clear Vic's hysterical rampage from my mind. "I'll try out the new coffeepot Daddy gave us for Christmas."

Bob laughed and wagged his finger at me. "Correction, my dear. He gave it to us the day *after* Christmas. Don't you remember? He wanted to commemorate the day the first percolator was patented. I'm getting used to his off-the-wall holidays."

"Yeah. How could we not know December 26th was such an important day? Do you want regular or one of the flavored varieties?"

"Whatever has the most caffeine. And if you have trouble measuring, err on the heavy side, okay?"

"I can make a pot of coffee." I stuck my nose in the air, feigning disgust.

"Oh, your coffee's wonderful when you remember to use a filter. The time you put the grounds in the basket without the filter—not so good." He smacked my rear and I headed for the kitchen.

I slumped at the table, coffee in hand, as Bob popped opened a can of instant sweet rolls. "Thanks, hon. Great idea." I needed the burst of energy the gooey icing would provide. "Before we eat, why don't you bring Bowie downstairs?"

Without a word, he walked upstairs and returned with the pup, bed and all, and placed her by my feet. He finished the sweet caramel rolls and iced them with the pre-packed mixture of gooey confectioner's sugar and joined me at the table. "What a mess." His voice sounded lifeless and his hair looked tousled from a restless night—grayer than when I met him less than a year ago. "I wonder where the hell Blane went. I'll have to tell Stan about Robin and that will bring out the whole sordid pile of shit."

I reached across the table and placed my hand over his. "You've been through worse, hon. I remember when you stood before the Senate Chambers and held your ground. You're the strongest man I've ever known."

"But what do I say? 'Hey, Stan, how's the last day in office goin'? I was wondering if you'd push a pardon on through for my biological mother. She's a lifer for prostitution and possession of coke. She didn't do it, but my dad, who by the way is John Gaynor, paid Blane MacGowan to send her down the river. She overheard some dirty dealings down in Texas and he wanted to keep her safe. In reality, he wanted to keep her mouth shut so he and *I* would be safe.' How's that sound?" He looked at me, then pulled his hand from mine and ran it through his already wayward hair.

I walked behind him and rubbed his neck and shoulders.

"That feels so good." He twisted his neck from side to side. I heard it crack—releasing the built-up tension.

"At least you know you can trust Stan. Better than having to go to Parsons with all this."

"Parsons. He might already know all of this. Remember, Blane visited him and they discussed Robin. How far it went, or what was exposed, I don't know."

I kissed the top of his head and refilled his coffee.

"Beth, do you think I'm doing the right thing? If I go to Stan, there's no turning back."

"What do *you* think? No. What do you *know* is the right thing?"

"You're right. I know what I have to do. It's not right that Robin was put in prison. I need to see Stan, then drive to Plymouth."

I smiled. "See? The answer was inside you all along."

"All this pondering's made me hungry again. Want another sweet roll?"

"Sure. Then we'll get a move on."

He reheated the rolls in the microwave—just a few seconds' worth.

The aroma filled the kitchen. Bowie's nose went straight up in the air as she whimpered.

"Hon, I think she's having a tough time getting up." I bent down and tried getting her to stand on three legs—she wobbled and lay down.

Bob rubbed her sides and coaxed her to hobble with a piece of an iced caramel roll. "See? She's fine. She's not used to smelling good food." He winked.

Ignoring his latest gibe, I said, "Let's take her for a walk."

"Don't you mean a hobble?"

I picked Bowie up and said, "Your daddy's a real clown, isn't he?"

She yawned.

I looked at the pup and asked, "Out?" She barked, I presumed in the affirmative.

"I think she's learned her first English word. That's the second time she's responded to *out*." She barked again.

Bob attached her leash and said, "Thank God we live in the middle of nowhere."

We put coats over our pajamas, slipped boots over our slippers, and headed toward the back door. The phone interrupted us again.

I looked at the caller ID. "It's Vic. You take Bowie, I'll be right there."

"No problem. My ears can't take much more of her rants."

I answered and all I heard was, "I'm coming over. I don't want to be alone on New Year's. He's such a pig."

I listened as she explained how she attempted to call his cell phone and he didn't answer. She surmised he was ignoring her.

"You'd better leave soon, Vic. We're heading to Lansing this morning." I told her about the meeting with Parsons and invited her to join us. I failed to mention Stan and the possible pardon. At least this time she said, "Okay, bye" before disconnecting.

Bob, Bowie, and I prepared for our day trip. We packed plenty of treats and water, her bed for comfort, and an extra blanket. Even though we'd been awakened at four, we still ran late. Bob called Stan and explained how having an invalid pup slows your routine.

By the time Victoria arrived, we were finally ready to hit the road. I opened the door and there she was, on our porch, holding a vase of pink roses. The ribbons were adorned with dog biscuits. "Oh my word, Vic, how adorable!" I took the arrangement and placed it on the coffee table.

"The delivery truck damn near ran me over in the driveway."

Bob walked into the room, unleashed Bowie and said, "Wow. Look at that! Thanks, Vic."

"Sorry. Not from me. A delivery. Cute driver, too." Even when dismayed over a missing lover, Vic notices.

"Early for a floral delivery, isn't it?" Bob asked.

"It's a *holiday*," Vic huffed. "They start early on *holidays*."

The way she emphasized *holiday* demonstrated Vic's typical dramatic approach to the English language.

"I signed for them," she said.

Bowie, sniffing out the treats, limped her way to the table, jumped with her two hind legs, and knocked the vase to the floor with her cast. Water splashed, glass broke, and Bowie, lying in the mess, chewed on a biscuit-adorned ribbon.

"*No! No no mal perro!* Bad dog!" I scolded.

Bob tried to disengage the pup from the mess. Victoria laughed.

"Well, who *are* they from?"

I found the card in the rubble. I read the outside of the envelope. "*To My Grandpup.*"

Bob smiled. "My first guess, with that note, would be your father."

Inside, the note read, "Happy cast day. I made that up myself. Sorry I don't know Spanish. Love, Grandpa."

"He's too much," Victoria said. "Maybe you two should have a baby. I mean—sending flowers to a *dog*?"

"What's wrong with that?" I asked. "Poor thing has a broken leg."

Victoria smirked. "I guess nothing. Here." She reached in her pocket and pulled out a pink sock, tied in a knot. "It's all I could find on short notice. The other half of the pair is in my drawer if she destroys this one."

I hugged her. "Awwwww. That is so sweet. Bowie! Look what Auntie Vic brought you."

"Wait a minute here. That's not from me. It was Pookie's idea."

"Oh," Bob said. "It's not okay for Beth's dad to send flowers but it's all right for a cat to send a pink sock. Makes sense to me."

I put the gift down by Bowie's mouth, but she shoved it aside. She was still involved in destroying the ribbons.

"We'll take it with us." Bob said as he grabbed the bags and her bed. "Honey, you take Bowie and, Vic—would you mind locking the door for us?"

Vic chuckled. "*Now* he remembers. About time, Larken."

As we walked to the truck, Vic asked, "Where do you think Blane went? It's not like him to run off."

"He didn't run off, really. He just needed a day or two to sort things out. He could be in real trouble if this gets out," Bob explained.

"Good point. He must have been real jittery to start smoking. He knows I hate it. I don't allow him to smoke in the apartment. What puzzles me is I called his brother— and his own brother doesn't know where he went."

Bob opened the passenger door and helped me settle in with Bowie. He got in and started the engine—a hint that we should discuss this later.

"Vic, leave that cell phone turned on and keep it charged. Have you checked your voicemail lately?

She looked at me with a blank face. "No."

Bob shook his head. "Have you had your cell phone on all the time, Vic?"

She put her hands on her hips and cocked her head. "No. I've been home. He'd call the apartment number."

"My God, are you sure you're not really blonde?" Bob asked. "Pookie knocked the damn apartment phone off the hook. If the cell phone was off . . ."

"Aw shit." She reached into the side pocket of her purse for her cell phone. She dialed her voicemail number, inserted her password, and listened. Her face turned white and she bit her upper lip. She looked up and said, "There was a message. It was date-stamped shortly after midnight."

I looked at Bob, and back to Vic. "That's when your apartment phone was off the hook. He must have called you, left the message, then called John. What did he say?"

"Nothing. There was a cough and then nothing." She stood, motionless.

"Vic, give me the phone. Don't touch any of the buttons." She handed me the phone and shuddered.

I looked under Recent Calls. "Vic, is Blane's number 555-4034?"

"Yeah. Why?"

"That call was from him." I showed Bob the readout and handed the phone to Vic.

"Listen, do not erase that message. Don't erase the incoming call log, either."

"Why?" she asked.

"I don't know. Just because."

Bob turned the heater higher and said, "Okay, I hate to do this but we need to get to Lansing. Vic, you coming?"

"Sure, I'll follow you," she answered.

We turned onto the main road and Bob said, "You've been watching too much Magnum P.I. You don't really think there's something wrong, do you?"

"Well, do you know there's not? It seems pretty fishy-most to me."

"Fishymost? Oh, that's a good one." His hearty laugh let me know he wasn't concerned about the aborted phone call Vic received.

"You have to admit it's weird."

"And what's *normal* for Vic's life and loves?"

I leaned my head back and snuggled Bowie close to my chest. "Want me to call Stan and let him know we're on our way?"

"Good idea. We'll only be another ten minutes."

I dialed the governor's direct line. He picked up on the first ring. "Well, you're quick today. Must not have much going on, huh, Governor?"

He explained that he was still in charge—still the governor. It was a good thing, too, he said, since no one had seen Parsons this morning.

"Well, it's still early, Stan." He continued explaining how they had a meeting set for seven with the Parole Board. The first round of recommendations. Public hearings had already occurred. Parsons wanted to sit in to view the process. They met without him.

I told the governor we'd be there shortly, to add Victoria's name to the gate guard's list of approved visitors, and hung up.

"That's strange," I said.

"Now what?" Bob asked.

"Parsons is a no-show today."

"He probably had too much pizza last night. He's sleeping it off. Is Shelly around?"

"I didn't ask. But first Blane and now Parsons. I don't like this."

"Well, just hold tight to Bowie. We don't want her to be next."

"Listen, remember what Vic said about Margaret? About revenge from the dead and all that? You think there's anything to that?"

"What—like Margaret's orchestrating disappearances from the depths of hell? You can't be serious."

"I don't know what I am—other than spooked."

We turned into the parking structure. Vic followed. Bob showed the attendant his identification and we headed to the visitors' area of the garage and parked. I put Bowie into her soft-sided carrier and walked with Bob and Victoria to the underground entrance of the Olds Building, where the executive offices are housed.

Once inside we were met by Lydia, whose eyes fixed immediately on the pup.

"What's with the cast?"

"An accident," Bob said. "She was about to be Maced so I tossed her in the back seat. Guess she landed wrong."

"You broke your dog's *leg*? Oh Bob, that's awful!" Lydia said. "Who was going to Mace her? Let me guess. You pulled up next to a mail truck, she stuck her head out the window, and went ballistic."

"Not exactly, but close. It's a simple fracture—she'll have the cast a few weeks."

"That's so sad, poor thing." Lydia stroked Bowie under the chin. "You three ready to party tonight?"

Victoria shot her a look that would convince Barbara Walters to shut up, then walked to the bathroom.

"Guess no word from Blane."

"Not yet, but he tried to call Vic. John, too. He must be in a bad reception area," Bob said.

"At least he tried. That must count for something," Lydia said.

"Not when it's New Year's Eve and your date is missing." As I finished my sentence, the bathroom door opened.

Vic stuck her head out and asked, "Either one of you have a lighter shade of lipstick? The shade I have is all wrong for this time of day."

I handed Bowie and all of her paraphernalia to Bob and whispered, "I know what she's doing. Fluffin' 'n buffin' in case Blane shows up."

Vic's voice raised a notch. "Well?"

I put my purse on Lydia's desk and rummaged inside. "You're in luck! I even have an extra lip brush—never used!"

As I pulled the small plastic case from my purse, Lydia said, "I had one just like that. Misplaced it somewhere."

"Didn't Thorne tell you? Bowie dug it out of a snow-drift. It must have fallen when the trash collectors dumped the garbage can into their bin."

"Yeah, I wouldn't let her throw something that valuable back in the trash," Bob joked.

Lydia grabbed the bag. "Well, then, it must be mine. I noticed it was missing right after we left your place. I'll keep it in my desk." She yanked the bag from my hand and shoved it in her top drawer.

Vic yelled, "Can I *please* have that lipstick?"

I walked into the restroom, purse over my shoulder, and said, "Man, Lydia came unglued when she realized that bag with the lip brush was hers. I guess it fell out of her purse when they were over at our place."

"Can't blame her for wanting it back. You can never have enough of those things."

"Yeah, but she lunged at me when she saw it. I mean, geeeez, it's just a stupid giveaway," I said.

"I could have used it, too," Vic sighed, as she freshened her face for a man who was missing.

CHAPTER 17

It is entirely amusing how many different climates
of feelings one can go through in a day.
—*Anne Morrow Lindbergh*

As we left the bathroom, something crashed. Lydia's high-pitched scream filled the hallway. We ran to the desk and found Bob on his hands and knees brushing a pile of mixed nuts and shattered glass from the floor.

"What on earth happened?" I asked.

Bowie whimpered and shook under Lydia's chair.

"One guess." Vic rolled her eyes and looked at Lydia. "It was the dog, right?"

"Bob was going in to talk with the governor. He gave her to me while you were in the bathroom."

"And?" I asked.

"She just dove for the nut dish."

"Oh, poor thing." I extracted her from her hiding place and snuggled. "It's okay. Shhhhhhhhh."

"I think it was the almonds," Bob said. "You know how she loves them."

"We'll replace the candy dish, Lydia. I'm so sorry," I said.

"It can't be replaced. It was a crystal dish we had made as gifts for the last inauguration."

"Oh, come on," Vic said, "you must have extras that you didn't give away."

"It's not important. As long as no one's hurt. Let me check her paws," Lydia said.

Lydia took Bowie's paws, one by one, and checked. "No blood. I don't see any glass between the pads."

"She's a bit clumsy with that cast. Her balance is off, " I said.

Stan came from the opposite direction and greeted us. "What happened to the dog?"

"Broke her leg," Bob said.

"I see that." Stan laughed and rubbed Bowie's ears. "We ready to do some last-minute business, Bob?"

"You bet. How does it feel, knowing you're soon to be a private citizen?"

Lydia answered, "Stupid question. With Parsons taking over, it feels like hell. A living hell. That man—"

"Yeah, we know how you feel, Lydia," Vic said. "He'll make great fodder for the late-night talk shows." She wrapped her lower teeth up onto her upper lip and knawed, imitating the way Parsons chews his moustache.

"Y'all are incorrigible," Bob said. "Have some respect. He's gonna be our governor."

"I think he's trying, I really do. He's become softer," I said.

Lydia protested. "You only say that because he offered you a job." She opened the bottom drawer of her desk and removed a can of mixed nuts. "Anyone want a handful before you start your meeting?"

Bowie pushed away from me—her nose pointed at the can. I sifted out a few almonds and put them in my coat pocket. Breaking one in half, I said, "Here ya go. Is that what all the fuss is about?"

"Nothing dainty about her eating habits. She didn't even chew that thing," Bob said. "Now that she's happy, let's get this over with."

Bob winked at Vic. "Why don't you stay out here and keep Lydia company. Make sure she doesn't exact bodily harm on our new governor when he arrives."

"Speaking of harm," Lydia said, "Have you seen that poster he has from the saloon in the Irish Hills? It's a black and white picture of just his face. It says WANTED—DEAD OR ALIVE. I've been tempted to take a marker and cross out 'or alive.'"

"Lydia!" I exclaimed, "That's awful!"

She shrugged. "So pray for me."

We entered an office filled with boxes and files.

"Have a seat, you two." The governor turned to Bob. "What's this about a pardon?"

"Do you remember when Blane was about to step down—he made headlines with that sting—the prostitute caught with cocaine?"

"That was the one called 'The State Bird Case.' I have a file on that."

"You do? What file?" Bob asked.

"The one John and I discussed yesterday."

Bob jumped to his feet and yelled, "What? What does John have to do with this? What did you discuss? What file?" His face turned red and the veins protruded on his neck.

"Cool down, honey," I said. "Let Stan finish."

"How do you factor into this case?" Stan asked. "Why the sudden interest? Has John been threatened? Level with me, Bob."

Bob walked across the floor and stood in front of the governor, his hands planted on his hips, "I want to know, and I want to know now, what John said," Bob demanded.

The governor responded, "He called me yesterday, then came to the office." Stan squirmed in his chair.

Bob took a deep breath before continuing. "Do you know John's my biological father, Stan?"

The governor looked out the window, averting his eyes. "Yes, yes I do. He came to me when Margaret died. He gave me a file and asked a favor."

"Damn it! He didn't tell me you knew. Why the hell did he do this?"

"He knows he can trust me, first off. I don't want to know particulars. I can't. I'm the governor. If I'm ever called to testify—concerning . . . anything—I have to be in the dark. When I'm asked if I know anything, I must be able to swear, on the Holy Bible, that I don't. You do understand that, don't you, Bob?"

Bob stared at the governor, his face expressionless.

"Bob, you know I want nothing to do with that fraternity. I won't be bought. I won't have my scruples questioned. The fraternity—those who are the secret keep-ers—they keep silent when they should take a stand and speak. You know that better than anyone."

"I'm not questioning your principles, Stan. I'm questioning John's."

I'd kept quiet long enough. "I don't suppose you'd tell us what that favor was, would you?"

He turned toward me. "John said if anything happened to him, I should push the paperwork through."

"What paperwork? Can we just get this out on the table, please?"

I was growing impatient. "Blane is missing, Parsons hasn't shown up this morning, and now we find out John—"

The governor interrupted. "He had everything in order. I was to be the executor of his estate. The Parole Board reviewed a clemency application made on behalf of—let me take a look here."

He removed a key from his pocket and unlocked a file drawer. He thumbed through several manila folders, then said, "Here we go. Robin Leeder. That's the one."

He placed the folder on top of the desk. "Is John alright? Why all this talk about him?"

Bob returned to his chair. "Would it be possible for you to pardon Ms. Leeder, Governor?" Bob asked.

"Everything is in order. All I need to do is grant it."

I glanced at Bob and said, "One signature and she'd be free?"

The governor took the file and tapped it on the desk. "Why does this concern you, Bob? John specifically said 'if anything happens to me'—so why now?"

"The paperwork's all there, right?" I reached for the file.

The governor pulled it away from me and said, "Yes. She's been a model prisoner. She's passed all of the psychological testing. She's no harm to society. It appears, in this instance, our rehabilitation program worked."

Bob coughed. One of those nervous coughs you get when you're trying to figure out what to say. "Stan, what I'm about to tell you—the part that I'm about to tell you—Robin Leeder is my biological mother."

"Holy Mother of God."

I motioned for Bob to join me. I held his hands and prayed. "Like Christ unjustly condemned. . . . grant that lawyers and judges may imitate you and achieve true justice for all people. Amen."

He smiled and said, "I know that one. The prayer's to Saint Thomas More."

I returned the smile and squeezed his hands. "It'll be okay," I whispered.

Stan looked across to Bob and me. "She—Robin—and John . . ."

"I don't want to go into that. It's not important. What's important is that she doesn't belong in Plymouth." Bob approached the governor. "Stan, you've been like family to me. Your son was a college chum. I need this favor, please," he begged. "Will you sign the paperwork? Can I go to Plymouth for Robin?"

"Bob, did you just discover Robin's your mother?" Stan asked.

"Yes, yes I did. John told me some things concerning Blane. I don't want to involve you in that. I can't. But trust me, Robin does not belong in prison."

"I don't need the media snooping around and digging up any wrongdoing. Is this on the up and up, Bob? Will I be sorry I did this?" Stan asked.

"Your meeting with John should probably stay between these walls." Bob said. "I'd simply say you had the paperwork and it got lost in the shuffle—bureaucratic red tape. Something other than John."

"You'll let John know this, right? I don't want to leave office and wind up in the headlines again. My administration has been flawless."

"And it will stay that way. That's why I can't answer any more questions, Stan."

The governor extended his right hand to Bob. "We'll shake on it."

"Thank you, Stan. Thank you," I said.

Bob took Stan's hand. "The media will have a field day with your last-minute commutations and pardons. The State Bird Case made quite a splash, just because of her name, so when it comes out that she and I are connected . . ."

"Bob, you know I would never discuss any of the individual cases with the media."

"They'll ask," I said. "They'll dig up everything on every case, you know that. This was a high-profile case. If Blane doesn't return before Robin's released, I'm not sure what spin they'd put on it. You can bet it wouldn't be a good one."

"Your mom and dad have been gone a few years now. And look—a second family. Your folks were wonderful people, Bob. They'd be happy for you."

Bob's eyes glistened and a tear fell down my cheek. Stan buzzed Lydia. "Can you bring me a black ink pen, please? I have one last order of business as governor."

CHAPTER 18

Be silent and safe—silence never betrays you.
—*John Boyle O'Reilly*

Governor Melvin buzzed Lydia's desk again. "The pen?"

The door creaked and Lydia entered. She pirouetted and showed off her new look. "Nothing much to do, so Vic gave me a mini-makeover."

"Yeah, but she wouldn't let me use that cute little brush," Vic pouted.

"I want to give it to my niece," Lydia said. Her eyes widened, or was that from all the eyeliner? "My brother's daughter—up in Traverse. I send her things like that from time to time."

I hadn't heard her mention that before, but I wasn't about to argue on such a special day.

As she walked past me to hand Stan the pen, Bowie let out a fierce bark.

"What was that all about? She damn near jumped out of your lap on all threes," Vic joked.

Lydia came closer—Bowie barked again, this time her nose twitched.

"*Cuál es incorrecto, muchacha*? What's wrong, girl?" Bob asked.

As Lydia approached, she extended her hand. Bowie sniffed it and stuck her snout into Lydia's blazer pocket.

"What's with this dog?" Lydia laughed.

"Do you have almonds in your pocket?" I asked.

Before she answered, Bowie pulled her nose out—her mouth firmly clamped onto the plastic bag that held the lipstick brush. Lydia pulled Bowie's teeth apart and yanked the pouch from the pup's mouth. "I was going to take this home. Control your dog, would you?" she snapped.

"Sorry," I said. "It's just a makeup case. She was looking for more nuts or a treat, that's all."

"Then give her a treat. This is an expensive jacket."

I looked at Bob and shrugged. Lydia placed the pen on the desk, stalked out, and closed the door.

"What was *that* about?" Vic asked.

"She's really on edge about being unemployed, I guess." I adjusted Bowie so she could look over my shoulder and out the window.

"Well, you two finish your business with the governor. I'm going to try Blane's number again." She left, and Stan smiled.

"Come over here—witness this close up."

I placed Bowie on the floor and we joined Stan at his desk. With a flourish of the pen, the governor announced, "I've freed the state bird."

Bob grabbed me. We hugged and kissed and turned to Stan. Bob pumped his hand—one of those handshakes that go on forever. I kissed Stan and thanked him again.

"Got any champagne?" Bob beamed.

"That's tonight, sweetheart. We'll have plenty to cele-brate, won't we?" I kissed Bob again. He picked me off the ground and twirled me.

"What now?" I asked.

Stan said, "I'll get the paperwork faxed to the prison. They go through everything, and she's released. I'll make some calls to speed the release. You can drive to Plymouth whenever you'd like. She should know by the time you get there."

Bob turned toward me. "What a New Year's gift this is! Everything's in order at the barn. She can stay there, right?"

"Sure, if she wants to. I don't know where else she'd go, and we have plenty of room."

Bob rubbed his hands together. He does that before a brainstorm. "I have that condo near Grand Rapids, the one John bought me before we got married. What do you think about me signing that over to her?"

"Great idea. That would put her near a city and still near us!"

Bob tilted his head. "Maybe she'd rather head back to Texas. I never found out if her family is still alive—if she has siblings—whatever. Come to think of it, I never found out anything."

"She might want to go home. We could let her stay at the cabin, couldn't we?" I asked. "It's not too far from Austin and close enough to San Antonio if her family is still around there."

Stan closed Robin's file. "Looks like you two have a lot to figure out."

"Sure do. Guess we need to take one step at a time." Bob's foot began tapping, his knee jumping up and down. Another nervous habit. "First step is meeting her. Can you imagine? I've never even met my mother—well, my biological mother—and here I am, deciding where she should live. *"*

"Why don't we let her make that decision? She's a free woman now."

Bob slapped his knee. "Well, I'll be go ta hell, she sure is!"

I couldn't believe our good fortune, yet the thought of taming Robin Leeder made me nervous. Her loud voice and abrasive mannerisms weren't what our friends would expect from Bob's mother.

"Stan, do you mind if we bring her by here later?" I asked. "We're starting the party at our house, then we'll come here for the stroke of midnight."

Bob laughed. "Thorne insists on being the one to pull Lydia away from her desk when the ball drops at Times Square."

Bob's smile caused a few well-earned crow's feet to form around his eyes. He twisted from side to side to loosen up his tightened muscles. The past few days had caused more than a few muscle spasms. "I need to call John."

"Here, use this." Stan moved the phone across the desk, removed the handset, and dialed 9 for an outside line. "It's a secure hard line. Safer than your cell phone."

Bob dialed and waited. "Hey, John, the governor has signed all the executive clemency papers. Looks like we'll be having a family reunion tonight. Call me."

He placed the phone back on its cradle and clapped his hands. "Won't he be surprised when he gets that message?"

The clapping startled Bowie, who barked once and fell asleep again.

"Do you think he'll be angry?" I asked.

"John has no room to be angry," Stan said. "He started this—we finished it."

"True." My overactive romantic gene got the best of me. "I can't wait to see John and Robin meet face to face tonight. I think she's still sweet on him."

"Oh, brother," Bob moaned, "here she goes."

"I'll shut up—for now." I flashed a toothy grin.

"I wonder where John is." Bob said. "He promised he'd call early this morning."

I cocked my head. "Yeah. That is strange. John always calls when he says he will."

"Excuse me, you two," Stan said. "I'll leave you with your thoughts for a moment. I need to expedite this paperwork so you can go get Robin. I'll be back in a few minutes. Would you care for some coffee while I make sure everything goes smoothly on their end?"

I looked forward to another caffeine boost. "You bet! Thanks. Bob, why don't you take Bowie for a walk? She hasn't done her business in awhile. I'll bring Vic up to speed on what's happened."

"Not a problem. I could use some fresh air."

"Hey, girl, what's going on?" Vic tossed her head back and shook her hair. "Man, it feels good to shake the cobwebs out. That Lydia's a strange bird. I had to pry words out of her mouth."

"Her job calls for her lips to be sealed. It's a carry-over. Don't worry about it."

Vic charged on as if I hadn't spoken. "Did you know she might move to Traverse City?"

I tried not to show my shock. "Last I heard she and Thorne were engaged. Why would she move to Traverse?

"Well, her brother lives there." Her eyes grew wide, as though she were divulging a deep, dark secret. "He's having some trouble with the little missus. Did you know that?"

"No, can't say I did."

"So, when they were up there, Thorne watched the kids and she tended to their shop while they went to a shrink. Isn't that a hoot? Lydia in a real job?"

"Vic, being the executive assistant to the governor is a real job." I laughed.

"Not really. It's a glam job. There's a difference."

"Apparently. So why do you think she's moving to Traverse?"

"I think I trapped her. I said 'Wouldn't it be nice if you could go up and help your brother out some—till he got his life back on track?' and she said 'It sure would be.' I'm telling you, she's moving up there."

"Vic, did she say she was moving to Traverse?"

"No. Not exactly. But she intimated. That's enough for me to know there's trouble in the future for her and Thorne. Count on that. Woman's intuition."

"Let's not start any nasty rumors, okay?" Sometimes the thought of muzzling Vic is attractive.

"So what was the big deal with the governor, Chrissy?"

I glared at her.

"You're still Chrissy to me—spill it."

I gave her the condensed version. I should have marked the day on Stan's calendar. "The day Victoria Marie Wexford was speechless."

"So when do we leave?" she asked.

"You can come with us to Plymouth. Leave your car here. You can sit in the back with the pup. Once we get Robin, I'll join you and let her ride up front."

"Sounds like a plan. Won't Blane crap when he finds this out? Serves him right for leaving me in the lurch on New Year's. The pig."

Her rant continued. "Yeah. He threw her in the pokey and now she's getting sprung. Jerk. That case was so weak."

"Not really. She was in possession of cocaine."

"Yeah. I believe that." She flashed me a grin, picked up a piece of scrap paper, and scribbled me a note. She passed it to me and said, "Just like in grade school. Here ya go."

It read, *The room could be bugged, right?*

I crumpled up the note and said, "You're too much, Vic. Listen, I need your help with Robin."

"How so?"

"Well, you know the makeover you did on Lydia? Think you could work your magic on Bob's mom before the party? I have a sneaky suspicion if she gets near makeup it'll be more than Daddy's heart can take."

"Yeah. That's right. In her younger days, she swung across bars. Oh, man, that's right, your dad—everyone will be there tonight. You got a saint for this? You're gonna need some heavenly intervention for this one."

CHAPTER 19

I like the dreams of the future better
than the history of the past.
—*Thomas Jefferson*

Once Stan assured us everything was set, we began our trip to Plymouth.

Vic's enthusiasm bubbled to the bursting point. "Oh my God, Bob, are you too excited, or what! Did you call John?"

"Tried, but no answer. He might be meeting with his CPA." He shook his head, grinning. "That's how he spent last December 31st. Figurin' and finaglin' those last-minute deductions."

"Yeah, no rest for the wicked, that's what they say." Vic laughed from the backseat of Bob's truck. She held a rawhide bone for Bowie to chew as they nestled together for the journey.

"Straight down Highway 127," Bob said. "It's an easy shot from Lansing. Hope the weather holds up. It was pretty nasty last night. Looks like they cleared the roads, though." He lowered his visor to block the morning glare.

Vic's mood had lifted for the moment. "This pup's kind of cute. She gets into some trouble, but she sure is loving."

"Yep," Bob said. "Just like her namesake."

I felt a story brewing. "Oh, do tell."

"It dates back to the Alamo. Austin thought Bowie was an impossible adventurer, but Houston saw Bowie's admirable qualities—a born leader and loyal friend. And there ya have it." He beamed.

Vic reached over the seat and patted the top of Bob's head. "And this pup even looks like she's been through a battle—cast and all. Thank you for that history lesson, Mr. Texas."

"Not a problem. 'Bout time you Yankees got a proper education." He started to hum *Texas, our Texas*.

"You got him goin' now, Vic," I laughed.

Bob wasn't about to stop the tale. "Another thing about Bowie, he was a real kind man. Once he intervened in a marriage ceremony . . ."

"Why the hell would he do that?" Vic asked.

"Well hush, now, and let me tell ya. He stopped the ceremony to save a young girl from marrying a well-known charlatan. Just the kind of man he was."

More *Texas, our Texas* humming. This time louder.

"He's on a roll, Vic." I said.

"Yep, those Alamo defenders, they had a fierce love of liberty. They knew it was the time to step up and take a stand to defend it."

I could hear Vic's dramatic yawn from the rear seat.

"Can't wait to put up that Lone Star flag you got me for Christmas, Vic. That'll look great at the cabin. I decided to place it directly outside the bathroom window."

"You *what?*" I asked.

"Yeah. That tall pole, what is it, something like twelve feet tall?" he asked.

"Something like that," Vic said with another yawn.

"We'll be able to sit in the bathroom and look up at that great flag."

I had to laugh at the thought. "You're too much, Larken."

Vic changed the subject. "You two ready for tonight? You didn't leave anything for the last minute, did you?"

"No," I answered. "Good thing—now that we're getting Robin."

"Hell of a New Year's present, huh, Bob?" Vic asked.

"More like hell of a New Year's *shock*." Bob reached over and stroked my hair. "Thank you."

"For what, sweetheart?" I took his hand, covered it with mine, and placed it back on the steering wheel.

"For believing in me. For meeting with Robin. For your support."

"You two." Vic sighed. "Well, I have a nice warm, cuddly dog next to me and my kitty when I get home."

That did it.

"Oh God." Vic sobbed. "Pookie. Blane gave her to me for Christmas."

"I don't have any tissue. Sorry, but here." I passed my scarf to Vic, who immediately blew her nose into the soft plaid fleece. As much as that sickened me, I knew she wasn't thinking clearly.

"You know what I believe?" Vic kicked the back of my seat. "I have been placed here on earth to have more heartache than a person should endure and I'm *pissed*. Whoever said life is a lemon is right. I want my money back!"

Another swift kick—this time with both feet. It felt like she was trying to kick her way out of quicksand. Maybe she was.

"Vic, there are no guarantees, and there's a no return policy." I said. "Right, Bob?"

"You shoulda read the fine print, gal."

He tried to lift her spirits. "Maybe it's time to move on, ya know? We'll ask Thorne . . ."

Her mood instantly changed. "Thorne? You think he knows someone? Someone that's as big a hunk as he is?"

Bob glanced my way, I winked at him and whispered, "Good call."

"Oh I'll bet," Bob said. "And Stan's son—he's older, my age, but he's single."

"He *is?*" One final nose blow into my scarf.

"Divorced. No kids," I said.

Her voice became excited. "I met him at the wedding—that's right. God, he's a *doll.*"

I was afraid the next thing my scarf would be needed for is drool.

We exited the expressway and Bob announced our arrival. "We're almost there! Vic, you're not on the approved list of visitors, so you need to wait in the car. You can tend to Bowie while we're inside."

"Okey dokey," she said.

A few turns and we were at the gate. We presented the guard our identification, she checked the roster, and noted Vic wasn't on the list. "She'll have to wait outside."

"Yes, ma'am," Bob said. "We're aware of that. It's not a problem. We've come to pick up a new release. I hope we won't be long."

"That's fine." The guard opened the gates and we were on the home stretch.

We announced our presence to the appropriate personnel and waited in the lobby area as they processed Robin's release.

"Do you think this will take long?" I asked a matron.

"Might. Never know."

I turned to Bob. "Did you leave the keys in the car? I think I'll call Vic and tell her what's going on. She can go get a cup of coffee in town if she wants."

"Yeah, then we can call her to come back for us."

My brain went into hyperdrive. "I wonder where Robin's clothes are. We might need to take her on a quick swing through the mall for a few things. I know she'll want some real food. That's one thing she complained about when I was here yesterday. She wants a Tex-Mex fix."

"Not a chance of finding that around here," Bob said. "She'll need to wait until I can make some of my killer nachos."

"I'll leave the cooking to you."

"Good call, hon." Bob grinned then looked around at the sterile walls and sparse furnishings. "I can't believe this." He squinted his eyes. "I visited a few prisons during my broadcast days. Have you ever been in one before?"

"Can't say as I ever have—before yesterday. What gets me is the odor."

His nervous energy was evident as he paced the linoleum floor. He twisted his torso to the right, then to the left, then rolled his head around on his neck.

"A bit tense, honey?"

"I just don't know what to expect. What if . . ."

A booming voice interrupted. "Mr. and Mrs. Larken? Come this way."

I grabbed Bob's hand and we walked down the brightly lit hallway.

"Wait here, please." The matron opened a closet and handed Bob a sack. "These are Miss Leeder's personal belongings. The ones she had when she was booked."

Bob glanced inside.

"Don't worry. Everything's there. We keep a prisoner's items under lock and key unless a family member picks them up."

Bob pulled a long chiffon skirt from the bag, followed by a peasant blouse.

"Are you certain these are Miss Leeder's?" he asked.

"Absolutely. They were tagged immediately when she was processed." She turned and left.

"She won't be winning the Miss Congeniality contest," Bob said as he handed me Robin's belongings. "You'd better look through this. Female stuff, you know? I'm still not sure these things are hers. Look at this." He tossed the peasant blouse in the air.

The door swung opened as I said, "Looks like it could be your mother's."

"Damn tootin' it's yer mama's!" Robin entered with a flourish, threw open her arms, and smiled. Holding her wrists in the air she said, "You missed the ceremonial unshacklin'."

I nudged Bob. He fixed his eyes on the doorway and walked toward Robin. The tense moment was broken by her hearty laughter.

"Well, ain't you somethin'—you look more handsome than on TV. Lemme look at you."

He stood before her—like a child having his clothes inspected before Sunday school.

"Hi, Robin," I said. "You must be anxious to get out of here!" At times like this, I think the angels sprinkle people with stupid dust. Here we were—a pivotal day in our lives—and that's all I could say.

Bob grabbed her hand, held it for a moment, and said, "Well, Happy New Year!"

"And you were a politician? Ain'tcha gonna say somethin' like 'didn't expect such a gorgeous doll'?"

Bob gave her a bear hug and I said, "Let's go—we have a party to get ready for!"

Robin reached for the bag of belongings. "Lemme go to a real restroom first. Gotta get me dressed up!"

"We'll meet you in the lobby," I said. "I have a phone call to make."

"Gotcha!" She strutted, bag swinging off her arm, down the hall.

Bob smiled. "We have more than a party to get ready for tonight."

I kissed his cheek. "She has potential. Let's call Vic and have her get back here."

"Vic and Robin—now there's a duo." Bob led me down the hall and I placed the call.

"Vic—we're ready to leave . . . Alrighty, then . . . See ya in a few."

Robin turned the corner, ran up to us, and curtsied. One of those Texas dips. She smacked her lips together and said, "Love lipstick. Didn't know how much I missed the stuff." Her admiration for all things Avon was evident by the various shades of crimson adorning her face.

I hesitated kissing her. I feared being branded. I wonder if being nibbled by lips like this gave birth to the term "red-neck."

She turned to me and examined my face. "You could use a lil color on yer cheeks, sweetie. If you wanna borrow mine, it's a killer. Called *Bodacious Blush*. M'lipstick, here—lemme check. *Ruby Rapture*. Now ain't that a name?"

The matron behind the desk called out, "Sir, that was the main gate. Your ride is here."

"Okay, ladies, time to get to Grand Ledge!"

Robin gave a Queen Elizabeth wave to the prison. "Ta ta, y'all!"

CHAPTER 20

Adopt the pace of nature; her secret is patience.
—*Ralph Waldo Emerson*

When Vic saw us approach she honked, waved, and pulled her lanky body from the driver's seat. One arm was filled with pup, the other she extended to greet Robin.

"Well, aren't you the dandiest welcoming committee. Hi there, I'm Robin!"

Vic grasped Robin's hand, introduced herself, and said, "And this is Bowie Aloysia Dog, but trust me, you can call her B.A.D."

Robin let out a hearty laugh and kissed the dog—smack on the lips. Robin giggled like a teenager as Bowie's tongue washed her face. "You're so sweet I could eat you with a spoon, sugah!"

The pup wiggled and Vic handed her to Robin. "She's all yours."

"That's fine by me," Robin said, as she turned her attention to B.A.D. "We'll make ourselves comfy cozy."

Vic and I climbed in the backseat and Bob began the drive home.

Vic passed B.A.D.'s favorite toy to Robin. "Here you go, gramma."

"*Gramma?* This pup is your sweet angel, Bobby?"

My hand covered my mouth and I kicked the back of Bob's seat. When he turned, I saw his face was the exact same shade as Robin's Ruby Rapture lipstick.

Vic tried to hold her sarcasm at bay. It didn't work. "Yeah, *Bobby*, didn't you tell your mama about the dog?"

"Okay." Bob said as he accelerated. "Time for some ground rules. First of all, Robin, please call me Bob. I'm still in the public's eye—if you feel the urge to call me *Bobby*, would you mind doing it behind closed doors?" He attempted to maintain a sense of calm as he continued. "Vic, please don't call her *gramma*. Her name is Robin. Did I miss anything?"

"Excuse me, Bob?" I bit my lower lip. "I do think you missed something—the entrance to the expressway."

Once Bob got us headed in the right direction, Robin snoozed, B.A.D. snored, and Vic and I passed notes back and forth. Neither of us wanted to offend the latest addition to the family, but we needed a plan. Fast.

Ten miles outside of Grand Ledge, Vic needed a pit stop. Robin took B.A.D. for a walk while Bob and I discussed the remainder of the day.

"Vic said she'd take Robin shopping—get a few things in town, and get that makeup toned down."

"Good idea," he said. "I can't believe we're resorting to Vic for a lesson in decorum, but do you think she can do something?"

"She suggested a diamond-studded muzzle."

Bob ran his hands through his hair and leaned his head back. "I don't even want to think about her after a few glasses of champagne."

"I have a sneaking suspicion those two speak the same language. Vic promised to help. Plus, this will keep her mind off of Blane."

"True."

Bob's cell phone rang. "It's Stan. I should have called him to let him know everything went alright."

"So tell him now! Answer the phone."

"Hey, Stan. How's everything there?"

Bob paused. "Okay, sure. A half hour. Tops."

"What's going on?" I asked.

"Stan wants us at the capitol as soon as we can get there. He didn't say anything else. Only wants the three of us there."

"The three of us?"

"You, me, and Vic. No Robin. He didn't sound good, Beth."

"What are we suppose to do with Robin? Vic was supposed to take her shopping while we got ready for the party."

"Hell if I know."

We waited for Vic, Robin, and B.A.D. to return. "Listen, guys, change of plans. Bob and I need to go to the capitol to help with a few things before the inauguration tomorrow. Vic, Lydia called and asked if you'd give her a fresh makeover." I slapped Vic's leg and glared at her. She knew exactly what I meant—shut up and play along. "Robin, now that you're free I'll bet you're wanting to spread your wings. You can use my car to go shopping."

Before she could answer, Bob said, "I have an account at the dress shop in town—get what you need, okay? But don't spill the beans. We need to make a formal announcement—like a coming-out party for you."

Vic chimed in, "Oh, my gosh! Our own little secret until the big announcement!"

"I sure could use some new stuff. I don't have no pajamas, even. They have them kinda silk PJ's?"

"I don't know, but the Lansing Mall has everything," I said. "Have the gals at the shop direct you. It's just a few miles. You'll love it! In fact, here, take my cell phone to keep in touch!" I passed the phone over her shoulder.

"Daggum, this reminds me of Christmas—but a week late." Her voice cracked. "Thanks, you two. This is awful special."

Vic poked me in the thigh and gave me a *what the hell?* look. I whispered, "Later."

Robin tapped her right shoulder.

"Something wrong? You can adjust your seatbelt," I said.

"Nope. Thankin' m'angel is all. You know, I got me an angel sittin' on m'shoulder."

As we turned onto the road that leads to the house and barn, Robin leaned forward to get a closer look.

"Hot damn, looky here. A sign that even says 'Private.'"

Bob slowed and pointed out the window. "See that barn? That's ours. It's made into a little retreat."

Robin remained quiet, turning her head from left to right, taking in the sights of the woods surrounding our property.

"And here's our house," I said. "Bob's best friend built it for us."

As we pulled closer, I saw two boxes on the porch. I jumped out and looked at the labels. Both were addressed to Bowie Aloysia Dog. They had been hand-delivered.

"Bowie, look here!" Bob held her leash, walked her to the porch, and I began unwrapping.

Bob shivered. "Get inside, girl. I'm freezing."

"Come on!" Vic said. "Open the packages. I'm about to burst!"

I moved the boxes inside and called for Bowie. "*Venido aquí, muchacha*. Come here, girl!"

"*¿Usted habla español?*" Robin asked.

"Nope," Bob said. "She doesn't speak Spanish, but the dog does. Beth's learning. Don't ask."

Bowie limped over, sniffed at the pink box, and sat down.

"It's from Kathy and Ken at the Four Seasons Gift Shop," I said. "Oh my word, it's a mix for making home-made dog bones! And there's a dog bone cookie cutter, too. They are so sweet."

Bob laughed. "Something tells me Ken had nothing to do with that gift."

Bowie started scratching at the pink-papered box that sat next to me. She barked and scratched at the wrapping.

"One guess," said Bob. "I'll bet it's from The Peanut Gallery."

Robin asked, "The what?"

"It's the local candy store." Bob said. "The only thing that will get that dog barking like that are nuts. They roast their own. She loves 'em."

"You're right," I said. "They sent her a little pink box of almonds. The note says 'Feel better soon—Your Friends at The Peanut Gallery.'"

Robin started to cry. Gentle tears flowed and her crimson lower lip quivered.

"Are you alright?" I asked. "Did I say something wrong?"

"No. No. Nothin's wrong. I'm twitterpated, that's all. You know—shaky. Y'all have such a great life. Such good friends an' all."

"Maybe you'd like to rest," Bob said.

"Maybe so." She shrugged off her coat, kicked off her shoes, and lay down on the couch. The day looked like it was starting to catch up with her, too.

"I'll leave my cell phone and some money on the kitchen table for you." I said. "And Bob's credit card for the shop is right here. I'll make sure he calls and tells them to expect you, okay?" I drew a quick map from our house to downtown. "It's less than five miles. If you have any trouble, dial *star one*—that's Bob's cell phone. Will you be alright for a while?"

"Sure, honey. You kids get along now. I'll be fine."

I smiled. She said *fahn* the same way as Bob.

"There's food in the cabinets—please help yourself." I felt guilty leaving her alone.

"Robin, you stick with the basics—a nice black pantsuit, maybe." Vic said. "Something tailored to show off your shape and pretty hair, okay? And nothing loud. That would detract from your natural beauty."

Thank God for best friends.

With Robin safely tucked in at the house, we hit the road—again. Bob turned the radio on to his favorite station. Vic made a face when we heard a country-western tune crooning "Happy New Year, Y'all."

"What's up in Lansing?" Vic asked.

"No clue. Stan called Bob when you were in the bathroom and said we needed to get there."

"Luckily," Bob said, "Lansing is close."

"Damn straight it's lucky." Vic said. "I couldn't take a long trip with that crap blaring over the speakers."

Ignoring Vic's comment, Bob said, "Once we see what Stan needs, we can pick up some groceries before heading home."

"Pick up groceries in Lansing? No way," I said. "I'll only do my marketing at Felspauch. You know how I feel about keeping business in town."

"You're right," Bob said. "Fine—Felspauch it is."

The sun reflected off the snowbanks. The roads were clear with very little traffic. "Not many people out and about," I said. "Bob, Stan didn't give any clue as to what he wanted?"

"Nope. Not a word."

He turned the radio louder and began to sing. "Isn't it great hearing the countdown of music? The hundred best songs of the past year. Man, there were some great ones."

"Uh," Vic said, "that's the hundred best country-western songs. That isn't exactly the best songs all around."

"Don't start, you two," I said.

Bob sang for the remainder of the trip. He turned the heater up and rolled down the windows, letting his strong baritone voice boom for all to hear.

As we approached the Olds Building, I leaned over and turned the radio down.

"Hardly the way to announce our presence." I laughed. "I feel like we've worn a path to this place."

We turned into the underground garage, took our choice of parking spots, and walked to the entrance.

A pale, shaking Governor Melvin met us outside.

"Stan, what's wrong? Are you alright?"

"I needed some fresh air."

"Is Bitsy alright? I asked. "Parsons? What is it, Stan?"

"Yes. Yes." He looked from Bob to me and fixed his eyes on Victoria. "I don't know about Parsons—Bitsy's alright—but Blane MacGowan's not. He's dead."

Vic leaned into me, her body limp and shaking.

Bob grabbed my arm and mumbled "Oh, dear God."

I bowed my head.

The words flowed by rote. I chanted them—some aloud, others silently. "Lord, make me an instrument of your peace . . . where there is darkness, light . . . and it is in dying that we are born to eternal life. Amen." Tears stung my cheeks and reminded me that winter's revenge was upon us.

Bob stood tall and took command. "We need to get inside."

We followed him without comment.

As we passed Lydia's desk, I asked her to call John. "He needs to get to the capitol. Tell him *now*."

Lydia glanced across her desk to Victoria. "Are you alright?"

Vic remained silent, her hand covering her mouth.

"Lydia, can you take Bowie for a few moments? Here's her bed. Pet her now and then and say "*Buena muchacha*. That's a good girl." I sat Bowie and her belongings on the floor, not waiting for a response.

I grabbed a notepad and pencil from the top of her desk. "Thanks."

Stan opened the door to a vacant conference room near the governor's office. As we entered the room, Lydia looked at her boss and asked, "What's going on?"

"Hold all calls. The only people I'll talk with are the police. That's it."

"What about Parsons, Governor?"

Her question went unanswered.

"I don't want to go into my office—Parsons' office— he's remodeled already and I'm not sure . . ." Stan Melvin, Governor of Michigan for less than twenty-four more hours, banged his clenched fist on the mahogany-paneled wall. "Damn, damn, damn." He unplugged the small radio that sat near Lydia's desk.

The room held six chairs and an oval desk; everything else had been removed. As we sat down, Bob said, "Stan. What the hell is going on?"

"Wait, please." Governor Melvin shut the door, placed the radio nearby, and turned the volume to its highest level. "Push the table over by the window and pull the chairs together—into the middle of the room." No one was about to eavesdrop on this conversation.

Victoria's voice quivered. "Where was he, Governor? When did this happen? How?"

I placed the notepad on my lap and prepared to write.

"I got the call just before you arrived."

"Why did *you* get a call?" Bob asked.

"The police checked Blane's day planner. It was on the seat next to his body.

They called me because the police have Parsons."

"What?" I screamed.

"The police have Parsons. He was the last person to see MacGowan alive."

Chapter 21

Death cancels everything but truth.
—*William Hazlitt*

Bob kept his voice low, but the intensity remained. "Tell us everything—and I mean *everything*, Stan."

"There's not much to tell. They found Blane in a ditch down south—in the Irish Hills—about seventy miles from here."

"Oh God," Vic moaned. "That's where he always went to think. There's a bar he loves . . .We've been there together. . ." Her words subsided into gentle sobs.

I folded my arms around her. "Could someone get her some water, please? I have aspirin in my purse."

"I don't want aspirin—I want to know who did this."

Stan looked at Victoria. "No one said someone did this. Could have been suicide. We don't know."

Vic broke away from my grasp and turned on her heels. Staring at the governor, she wiped her eyes and gasped, "Suicide?"

"Please," Bob said, "let's try to think this through and not jump to conclusions. One step at a time. When did you hear about this, Stan?"

"Just before I called you. I hung up from talking with the Highway Patrol and Parsons, and dialed your number."

"The media," I said. "How is this being handled? You know they listen on the police band for accidents. They would have gone to the site."

"They did. I haven't had the news on this morning. I'm sure they ran the plates. It's public record. The media— that's another reason I wanted you here."

"Another reason?" I asked. "Why did I know there had to be more? Isn't Blane's death enough?"

"Well, there's Parsons," Stan said.

"Chrissy?" Vic looked at me, her face streaked with tears. "Can you write this all down for me? I can't think straight."

I began to take notes. "Alright. Spill it."

"When Blane's car was discovered, in a ditch, the Adrian police were notified."

"The Adrian police?" I asked.

"That's right. That's the jurisdiction—the closest police. They saw a day planner on the seat. Once they ID'd Blane, they knew this would be a major case. You know, his prominence."

"Yep. That makes sense," Bob said.

Stan continued. "They looked at the day planner, then tagged it. It was open to yesterday's appointments. They saw that the judge had been to see Parsons. That was the last entry. The state troopers arrived at the scene and phoned Parsons. Asked him to come to the trooper station in Jackson."

Bob stared at the wall. "Shit."

"A state trooper drove Parsons from his home to Jackson, of course." Stan cleared his throat. "Like I said, Jim was the last person to see Blane—that we know of, at least. Naturally they wanted to question him about that visit."

"Double shit." Bob lowered his head and rested it between his hands. "John said Blane came clean with Parsons. How would he know that if he didn't see or speak with Blane after their meeting?"

"Exactly my next point," Stan said. "They checked Blane's phone. A call was made to John after the appointment with Parsons. Then no further calls until much later. A call to John, but it was only a second or two."

"That's right," I said. "We were with John when that call came in. He knew it was Blane, but it was a disconnect. We thought it might have come from a poor coverage area."

"That's right," Vic sniffled. "Sometimes you can't get through when you're in the Hills. That would be right. And then he called me. Remember?"

Bob said, "Yep. Left a message. Not really a message, but it was him. Okay, Stan, what else?"

"I wasn't concerned when Parsons wasn't here early this morning. Figured he was working with his speechwriters for the inauguration tomorrow. Never did I think he'd be questioned in a death case."

"*What* case?" I yelled.

"Please, don't yell. We don't want anyone to get suspicious," Stan said.

"Hell, it's only Lydia. She's almost a member of the family, Stan," Bob said.

"Still and all, she's not privy to the details. She doesn't know what transpired between Blane and John. For that matter, neither do I. And I don't *want* to know. I'm going to leave this office cleaner than when I arrived."

"We know," I said. "Stan, maybe you should leave now. The three of us need to talk and if you're not here . . ."

Stan looked at me. "Like I said, I don't want to know."

Once the governor was out of the room, I sat Vic and Bob across from me. "We know John went to your place. John and Blane smoked. Blane and John each came to the capitol and spoke with Parsons. Blane—we're not sure why. John? To see what went on between Blane and Parsons."

"I think we can assume that Blane went to his friend, Parsons, because he's going to become the next governor. Maybe he wanted to see about pardons for some of the prostitute cases," Bob said.

"If that's true," I said, "why Parsons? Why wouldn't he go to Stan? The outgoing governor would be the best bet for a pardon."

Vic stretched her legs and rubbed her forehead. "Because he'd have to explain too much to Stan. Governor Melvin is squeaky clean. No way would he tell Stan he was bought. Hell, no one but John knew."

The door flew open. There stood Lydia with B.A.D.'s pink leash wrapped around her legs. "Sorry. I can't do this anymore. She's like a ten-pound steamroller and that cast should be on file as a lethal weapon. Here. Take her."

I walked over to the door and extracted Bowie from Lydia's legs. From the doorway, I could see the mess. "What happened?"

I stepped into the hallway, where Lydia's desk sits, and witnessed the ravages of Hurricane Bowie. "Sit." I commanded. The pup pulled in the opposite direction and fell into the remains of the trashcan.

Bob called from the doorway, "I think she's gotten her energy back."

Lydia looked at the jumble of papers. "I think she needs some training."

Vic stayed behind, but Bob wandered through the debris. "Here, let me take her. We need to finish and get some errands done."

As he picked up Bowie, Bob tilted his head. "What's this?"

He spread the soft, feathered hair apart on the dog's underside. "Come here, Beth, take a look."

Lydia frantically gathered the mess from the floor as Bob held Bowie in the air. I picked at the plastic entangled in a mat of hair.

"Pretty sticky. Looks like one of those smoker's patches," I said. "Lydia, what's this doing in your trash?"

She glanced up, shrugged, and returned to cleaning.

"Lydia?" I joined her on the floor and showed her the patch. "So?"

"I have no idea. Must be Parsons'. He probably threw his trash in my basket."

I glanced at Bob and motioned for him to go back into the conference room.

Lydia looked up from the mess and said, "All of you—just leave it be. I've got it, okay?"

Bob took Bowie, I took the patch, and we joined Vic, closing the door behind us.

"Your brain is working on overtime, Beth. What are you thinking?" Bob asked.

"I want to see if this is the same sort of patch Parsons uses and if the box we found is from the same make. There's a tie-in here, I know it."

Vic, her face streaked with mascara, asked, "And what does this have to do with Blane?"

I held the patch in my hand, turned it over, and said, "I don't have a clue, but I know it does. Trust me, I have a few questions for Jim Parsons. Bob, who would want Blane dead?"

"For starters—I hate to say this, but John. With Blane dead, his involvement with Robin dies, too."

I shook my head. "John is a wheeler-dealer. He's done plenty of unsavory things, but murder?"

"I know," Bob said. "I don't like to think that either. But we all know—"

"Parsons," Vic interrupted. "If Blane had something on Parsons and threatened him—hell, we don't know what they talked about."

"John said Blane came clean with Parsons," I said. "What does 'come clean' mean? Did he talk about the trials or something else?"

The door opened and Stan joined us. "Man, Lydia is one upset lady. She's out there cleaning like her name is Mrs. Hoover."

"Yeah," I said. "Bowie made quite a mess. Guess she attacked the trash."

"Oh," Stan said, "I thought it had something to do with Parsons. She was muttering and rambling on, cursing the day he was born—spouting off how our state is doomed— you know, the usual."

"Stan, we need to think this through. Ask some questions," I said. "Something isn't computing."

"Blane would never commit suicide." Vic started to sob again. "We had so many plans. He might have needed to clear his conscience some, but kill himself? I don't believe that."

Bob scratched his head and paced. "Okay. We're going back home. Vic, you need some rest."

"Rest? When Blane just got killed?"

"We don't know that yet," I said.

"I know it!" She yelled. "Don't try and tell me otherwise. Somebody ran him off the road. Poisoned his beer.

Something. I don't know." She put her head in her hands and wept.

"Stan, thanks for calling us. I'm glad we heard it from you rather than the news," Bob said. "We talked all the way to and from Plymouth, then had the radio on when we drove to Lansing, but not on AM."

"For once, thank God for those continuous music stations," I said.

Lydia knocked and didn't wait for a response. She walked in and said, "Bob. John's on the phone."

Stan asked Lydia to join us while Bob took the call.

Lydia looked at Victoria, then at me. "Something's going on. It's Parsons, isn't it? He's hasn't come in. He's dead, isn't he?"

Victoria looked up and hissed, "You wish."

Chapter 22

Men are not punished for their sins, but by them.
—*Elbert Hubbard*

"No. No, of course not." Lydia rubbed her hands on her skirt and adjusted her shirtsleeves. "I seemed to, well, you know—he's not around and everyone's upset. That's all."

I studied her face. A minor twitch—rapid eye blinking.

Why would Lydia be so uncomfortable? I wondered. Maybe the transition is getting to her. The inauguration is tomorrow afternoon and she'll be out of a job. Thorne makes good money, though. It's not like she'll need to work after they get married. She's fiercely loyal to Governor Melvin. They've been a team for years. I'm not sure what he'll do once this term has ended, but I can't imagine he wouldn't hire Lydia in some capacity.

"When was the last time you saw Parsons, Lydia?" I asked.

She stammered, "Um, well, let's see . . ."

This was a woman who's always in complete control. She knows every move in this building. It's her job to know.

"Lydia?" I asked.

"I'm trying to remember."

I moved closer. She backed away. A bad chess game. Who'd call *checkmate?*

This was strange, at best. Lydia and I were friends. Well, sort of. She's engaged to Bob's best friend—but we were on her turf. She's not accustomed to being challenged on her own ground.

"I remember," she said. "It was when John came by yesterday. No, it was Blane MacGowan. That was it. I took a cup of coffee into them. Imagine that. *Me* a gofer for that pig. Oh—sorry. I'm sorry." She hung her head. "I mean, with his death and all, I didn't mean to be . . ."

Vic leaped from her chair. "How did you know Blane died?"

Lydia's face went white. She grabbed my arm and gasped. "Blane? Died? What?"

Vic glared at Lydia, then at me. "What the hell is going on here? There's no TV or radio on. Who called you—Thorne? And why are you acting so surprised?"

"Oh God," Lydia moaned. "I assumed it was Parsons. Oh God, I didn't know."

I motioned for Lydia to take a seat. "His car went off the road," I said. "He was down in the Irish Hills. We don't know what happened. You stay here with the governor. We're going to take Vic with us—she needs some rest."

Lydia squirmed and wrung her hands. "Do we know what happened to Parsons?"

Bob had opened the door. When he heard the question, he responded with a firm, "No." He glanced around the room and said, "Vic, Beth—let's go. Stan, stay put."

Stan gave Vic a hug, patted the pup on her head, and kissed my cheek. I whispered, "Say nothing to anyone. And I mean *anyone.*"

"I'll be here the remainder of the day," Stan said.

Lydia stood, head erect, and said, "I'll be here 'til midnight, unless I'm needed longer."

We took our lead from Bob. I walked behind him, Bowie under my arm, with Vic on my left.

He was silent until we reached the car. "Beth, what was with the interrogation back there?"

My turn to give the orders. "Bob, turn on the car—blast the radio. Everyone in the backseat." I tossed my purse into the front of the truck.

The three of us, plus Bowie, scooted near one another on the bench seat of the truck. "Something is off—way off. Lydia is at her desk constantly, unless she goes to the bathroom. Why would Parsons remove an old smoker's patch at her desk and throw it in her trash? It must have been while she was in the ladies room. Otherwise, she would have mentioned it when we found the thing stuck to Bowie." My adrenaline surged, giving me that extra push—like athletes before the big game.

Vic sniffled and wiped her eyes. "What does that have to do with Blane?"

"I don't know. Bob, what did John have to say?"

"He'd heard the news—it's all over television. Blane was a prominent judge. I told John not to come to Lansing. No point now that we're heading home. Oh, he asked about Robin, or, as he calls her, Binnie."

"Oh no," I said.

I'd almost forgotten that little detail. "What are we going to do with her?" Dealing with Blane's death and entertaining Bob's mother simultaneously—quite a juggling act. No way could I handle being the ringmaster right now.

Bob's face registered no emotion. It was a blank slate.

"Bob?" I asked. "Did you hear me?"

"Sorry." He shook his head. "Need to clear the cobwebs. Way too much going on."

Vic stuffed the used tissue in her pocket. "No shit. You know, I could use a break. I can't sit around and cry all night. Robin can come to my place. She'll be a good diversion. She can watch me drown myself in a bubble bath."

My voice grew stern. "That's not funny, Vic." I tapped Bob on the thigh. "What do you think, honey? I hate to pawn your mom off on somebody else so soon, but—"

"Well, we didn't exactly know all the complications that would arise," Bob said. "It's not like we planned this."

I nodded. "No, we didn't plan this."

But, I thought to myself, somebody else might have.

Bowie started to snore. Vic stroked her tiny pink cast. "She's tuckered out.

Must be from her demolition derby routine. That can't be easy on three legs. Poor thing."

Before we left the parking garage, Bob called Thorne and asked him to meet us at the house. He'd heard the news and was worried about Vic. I called Daddy and told him our party plans were on hold. He understood, and assured me that his new vest would be ready to wear at a moment's notice.

Next call—Robin. She reported that she'd showered and raided my closet.

"Vic," I said after I got off the phone. "She's poured herself into my clothes."

"She *what?* Robin is wearing your clothes? You're joking."

"No, no joke. Bob, Vic and I will stay in the back. We have some strategizing to do." For the first time in hours, I laughed.

"While you two cook up whatever scheme is next, John had a generous offer."

Vic rolled her bloodshot eyes. "And what does *that* mean?"

"He suggested you take Robin to the Amway Grand tonight. He has a suite there, you know. Complete with a refrigerator stocked with soda and a freezer full of Pecan Delight Ice Cream. You can have room service or go to their New Year's bash."

"Don't you need tickets for that?" I asked.

Vic answered before Bob had the chance to respond. "You do unless you're John Gaynor."

"Are you up for it, Vic?" Bob's voice was soft and loving. Vic can be a handful, but she's loyal—a trait Texans worship.

"And what would be my choice—the bubble bath, alone? Count me in. And thank John for me, will you?"

"No problem," Bob said. "Now what's this about your clothes and Robin, Beth?"

"After her shower, she wanted fresh clothes. She ransacked my closet. Sounded like she had fun, too."

Vic smirked. "What on earth would she find in *your* closet that would fit? She would be better off with one of little *Bobby's* shirts."

I couldn't resist. "Girlfriend, there ain't nothin' little about her Bobby."

From the front seat came a booming voice. "You two are incorrigible. I'm not sure putting Vic with Robin is wise. That poor hotel."

"My turtlenecks," I said. "They'll be stretched out. She's a couple inches taller than me. My slacks will be high-waters. Oh, man."

"Let's get back to our plan," Vic said, as she opened her purse. "Oh, here, I thought you might want this. It seemed to intrigue you. Lydia pissed me off so I took it from her drawer."

She handed me the plastic case that held the lipstick brush. "You stole this from Lydia?"

"Well, when you put it *that* way."

Bowie went ballistic. Her jaws clamped down on the makeup case as she whipped her head back and forth.

"Damn. She loves that thing. She think it's a toy, or what?" Vic asked.

"Bowie, come on." I was exasperated.

I extracted the container from the Jaws of Life and tossed it over the seat. "Bob, put that in my purse. If it's on the floor, then shove it under the seat. Geeeeeez."

Bowie wiggled her way out from my grasp and dove for the front seat.

"Ten pounds of terror headin' your way, cowboy!" Vic said. "Not bad for a wounded warrior."

Bob rattled something off in Spanish, tapped the passenger seat and, struggling, Bowie made it over the headrests and lay down.

"Okay," I said. "We were talking about a plan?"

Vic's eyes became moist again. "I think we were *trying* to. I want to help with Robin."

"After we see what's she's helped herself to, wardrobe-wise, maybe you can drive her to the hotel. I know the concierge can help with clothes—they can do anything," I said. "Let her enjoy herself but, please, try and convince her somehow that she'll be in the public eye—I don't know how we can hide her."

"Hide her? That's an awful thing to say."

Vic was right, but imagining Robin with my father and John, Bob, Thorne, and the media . . . something had to give.

Vic sat for a moment. "If I could get her lipstick toned down—maybe tame her hair—get conservative clothes—I think she'd be terrific."

"You are hereby appointed the Ambassador of Makeovers," Bob said with a chuckle.

"Go ahead and laugh, Larken. You'll thank me in a few days!"

I looked at Victoria. "A few days? You've got less than twenty-four hours if the two of you plan to go to the inauguration."

"Oh crap," Vic said. "You're right. And I want to talk to Blane's brother. Find out the arrangements—you know."

I took her hand, squeezed, and said, "I know. I'd like to sit down and play the piano for days on end. Best way to relieve tension . . . but first I have some loose ends to tie up."

Vic and I sat there, hand in hand, as Bob traversed the final twists and turns heading to our house. As we pulled into the drive, the door flung open. Robin—wearing a purple knit sweater four sizes too small, a pair of stretch jeans that, on her, looked like capris, and my white fuzzy slippers—greeted us.

Bob, with Bowie in tow, opened Vic's door and said, "She's all yours."

"Oh, honey child, c'mere," Robin called to Vic. As Vic approached the door, Robin grabbed her and said, "Baby girl, I'm so sorry. Oh, this here's plum dreadful." She swayed back and forth, Vic limp in her arms.

"Thank you, I appreciate your concern," Vic responded.

"It's been all over the news. You kids, c'mon in here. I helped myself to the kitchen and baked us up some lil snick snacks."

Bob beamed. "Thanks—do I smell cookies?"

"You bet, baby boy. Them are those dog biscuits y'alls' friends sent over for the pup there. Also made some brownies. Ain't been in no kitchen for quite some time. What a treat!"

I hugged Robin. "Thank you, really."

"I had t'do sumthin to get m'mind off that horrible accident. A sin, I'm tellin' ya."

"Well, now we have a surprise for you," Bob said. "Vic is going to take you to her place in Grand Rapids then over to the Amway Grand for the night. You can have your own girl's night out!"

"The Amway Grand?" Robin's eyes widened. "Where y'all had yer reception? The one in that movie—was it *Dunston Checks In?* Yeah, that was it. Hot-damn! That's a first-class place."

Vic looked down at her feet adorned in my slippers. "We'll have to do something about shoes. You have anything with you?"

"I have m'heels. The ones I was wearing at the bar when they hauled me off. Didn't go with the jeans though. Wrong color. A girl's gotta match, yanno."

Vic looked her up and down. "Did you get into town?"

Oh God, I prayed. Please tell me she didn't go into town looking like that.

"Into town? I was too dern busy cookin'! I didn't know we was goin' to the Grand! I'da gotten me some new lipstick!"

"The Lansing Mall is still open," Vic said. "We'll leave now and pick up a few things." She looked at the slippers. "You can't wear those."

"Well, lemme put m'skirt 'n heels back on. It's all I got right now."

Robin went upstairs and we all stood and looked at one another.

"Please tell me you have a saint for this," Bob said.

Vic raised her hand. "Even I know that one. A no-brainer. Saint Jude. The Patron Saint of Lost Causes."

CHAPTER 23

The pure and simple truth is rarely pure
and never simple.
—*Oscar Wilde*

With Vic and Robin out of the way, I looked at Bob and asked, "What do you make of all this?"

"All of what? Meeting Robin once she was pardoned? Finding out Blane's dead? Discovering Parsons is being questioned by the state troopers? Wondering how my father figures into this—or the shock of seeing my mother in clothes that would make a circus clown proud? Take your pick." His voice, drenched in sarcasm, was cold and emotionless underneath. He leaned back, put his feet on the ottoman and clasped his hands behind his head. "Oh, by the way, Happy New Year."

"We need a chocolate fix."

I walked into the kitchen and cut two chunks of brownie from the pan, poured each of us a glass of milk, and returned to the living room. "Open wide, Mr. Larken. Nothing like a hunk of chocolate when you're pissed off or depressed."

"Oh no you don't. I have a good memory. I remember when you smashed a brownie all over my face. Not gonna let that happen again." He smiled and took a swig of milk.

The doorbell interrupted our brownie binge.

"I'll get it," I said.

I opened the door and was greeted by Thorne, a dozen yellow roses, and a pink teddy bear. "Oh you're so sweet! Thanks—let me take the flowers and put them in water. I love yellow roses—they symbolize friendship."

As Thorne entered, he shrugged off his jacket and left his boots by the door. "Sorry, they're not for you. The flowers are for Vic—I thought she could use a pick-me-up. The bear is for the injured member of the family."

He went to where B.A.D. lay and placed the bear on the floor next to her. "There ya go, girl. Your dad told me you've had quite the adventure."

She snored right through his well wishes. "I have a devastating effect on women, don't I?" Thorne laughed. "I take it the party's officially off?"

I returned from the kitchen carrying the flowers and a vase left over from our wedding. "Yeah, looks that way."

I inhaled the aroma of the roses. "When this is all over, I say we all head to the Hill Country. I haven't had a Texas fix in awhile. You and Lydia want to join us?"

"Sounds great to me. I'm not teaching this semester and Lydia will soon be unemployed."

I smiled. "We can sit around and make wedding plans."

Bob chimed in, "Girl stuff. Us guys will go riding, shoot some guns, look for a pickup truck—maybe a tractor."

Thorne nodded. "Yeah—testosterone overload. Count me in, pal." They high-fived and belched. Two grown, respectable, professional men. Disgusting.

"Now that your innards have been cleared, can we get serious?" I asked.

"Sure," Thorne said. "What's up? I take it this is about Blane's death."

I looked into his eyes. You can tell a lot about a man that way. He never flinched. "This is a real puzzle, Thorne. Maybe you can help make sense of this."

"Me? Why me?" he asked.

"Because you have no involvement in this," Bob said. "We, however, are knee deep in shit at this point."

Sitting around the coffee table, we ran through what we knew thus far. Thorne listened without comment. He's an attorney, I thought. He's also a professor. He teaches law at Grand Valley State—the same university where Bob's been an adjunct professor in political science. I prayed that his legal mind would help us sort through what was fact and what was supposition.

"Beth, do you have the cigarette butt, the patch, and the empty box?" Bob asked.

"I sure do. From what I can figure out, the butt is from John, but the patch and box are from Parsons. I can't figure out why the patch was in Lydia's trash can, though."

"Could be any number of reasons," Thorne said.

"Such as?"

"Well, maybe Parsons borrowed the trash can. Might have moved it into his office while he redecorated. Maybe he went to her desk to get something when she was at lunch and changed his patch. Could have been anything."

I thought about his ideas and asked, "Anyone know where he wears it?"

"I think his left arm," Thorne said. "He's left-handed— that I know. I remember seeing him rub his upper left arm. I asked about it and he said the patch was buggin' him."

"Man," Bob said, "you attorneys notice all the details."

"Got to," Thorne replied. "I teach my students that, too. Learn to watch everyone and everything. A minor detail can change a case. Have you found out why Blane went to see Parsons, or what John talked about with Parsons? Seems like the link is our soon-to-be-governor."

Bob groaned. "I was afraid you'd say that."

Bob told Thorne about Robin, Victoria's account of what Blane said in his sleep about "Binnie," and how he thought perhaps John might have influenced the trial. Knowing that Thorne is an officer of the court, he didn't go into detail. He explained how Robin and Vic were staying at the Amway—at least for the night.

"Seems like John might be another link," Thorne said. "Call him and get him over here."

Bob rubbed his hands on his jeans, then through his hair. "I . . . I was hoping we could discuss this without him."

"Is there something you're not telling me, old buddy?"

"Maybe so—maybe no. I'd really rather try this alone—for now at least." Bob stood and paced. "There has to be something we're missing." He picked up Bowie and placed her on the couch between us.

I opened my purse and pulled out my makeup kit. "This darn weather is really making my lips chapped. Sorry, fellas, I need a touch up."

Remembering that I had Lydia's lip brush, I pulled the plastic pouch from my bag. "This will work great with my lip balm."

Bob shook his head and smiled. "A guy is dead, Parsons is being questioned, and my wife is playing beauty parlor."

Without warning, Bowie stirred, put her snout in the air, and batted Lydia's pouch with her cast.

"She looks like a cat," Thorne said. "That's hysterical."

What happened next was not funny.

Bowie wailed. She howled. She growled and barked. She tore into the bag like it was filled with solid gold gourmet milk bones. Her teeth locked onto not only the bag but also my sleeve. I pulled back and the material ripped. She yanked. The fabric gave up. She won the battle of the blouse.

"What the hell got into her?" Bob asked. "What's with her and that damn bag?"

In a frenzy I tossed the pouch to Thorne, who caught it midair. Bowie tried to scurry off the couch. With only three legs it wasn't an easy task.

Bob reached over and grabbed her midsection. "Whoa, missy. *Consiga detrás aquí.* Get back here!"

Thorne looked at the makeup bag. "Lydia got one just like this when we went to visit her brother, up in Traverse City."

"That was recently, right?" I asked.

"Yeah. We went to help them out. Lydia tended to the store when they went for counseling. Nice people—hope it works out for them."

"What kind of store? I don't think you've ever mentioned it," Bob said.

"Her brother's a jeweler."

Something clicked when he said jeweler. Something I'd read about a jeweler being poisoned with a chemical he was using. It stayed with me because the chemical smelled like almonds. At the time I told Bob, "With the way our pup loves almonds, we better watch out."

I licked my lips. "Hey, Thorne, I hate to be an Indian giver but can I use that lipstick brush?"

I took it, turned toward the stairway, and smelled the brush. An unmistakable faint, bitter almond scent. That's why Bowie raised such a fuss. She smelled almonds!

"Bob, hold onto Bowie. I'll be right back."

As I headed upstairs I heard Bob mumble, "Women."

I yanked open the closet door and pulled out my laptop. My desktop computer was at the barn. I unplugged the phone and sat on the bed, computer perched on my lap. I muted the sound and attempted to dial into the Internet. Weird signal. I tried again—same thing. I checked the settings. The dial-up was set for an Austin access number. I changed it and a few minutes later I was logged on, surfing the Net. I searched almond-smelling poison—then almonds and jewelers. I took the information and cross-indexed.

Nitrotoluene—toxic by all routes—dermal absorption. It may be absorbed through intact skin—jewelers—sodium cyanide.

It was here somewhere. I searched further.

If slightly diluted, sodium cyanide crystals can be applied to a surface and transmitted through intact skin— Sodium cyanide is used to clean tarnish from gold and silver jewelry.

But Lydia? What ax did she have to grind with Blane MacGowan? It couldn't be Lydia. What was I missing?

I wrote what I'd discovered on a piece of scrap paper and tucked it in my pocket. Next, I locked the brush away with the cigarette butt, used patch, and empty box, then returned the laptop to its place in the closet.

"Beth?" Bob called from the living room. "What's going on?"

"Just wanted to try that brush out—I have some fancy beeswax lip balm upstairs. Works great!"

Smiling, I rejoined the men and pup and said, "Much better."

"I'll never understand women," Thorne said. "You called me out here to discuss Blane's death and you're worried about chapped lips."

I shrugged. "Did I hear your cell phone ring, Bob? I thought I heard you talking. Was it Robin?"

"No, it was Parsons. He said he wanted you to start working for him immediately. Guess your phone is turned off."

I looked in my purse. Sure enough. Dead battery. "Forgot to recharge it. Shoot. Good thing I didn't give it to Robin. Now what's this about me working?"

"Brace yourself," Bob said. "They're giving Parsons a polygraph. John's next."

"John? Oh no—" I thought about what I'd discovered and how it might tie in to either of these men. "What does Parsons want me to do?"

"He wants you to come to Jackson. The media hasn't found out, but if—when they do, he wants you there to handle them."

"Man," Thorne said, "Lydia's gonna love this. She hates that man."

I remembered my recent discovery. "Please, Thorne, let's keep this between these walls, okay?"

Bob looked at me as I bowed my head. I closed my eyes and breathed deeply. The men remained quiet as I recited, "Oh, Glorious Saint John . . . now on earth and forever after in heaven." As I lifted my head, I wiped a tear from my cheek.

Bob put his arm around me. "Are you alright? What was the prayer for?"

The tears flowed freely now. I looked at Bob, and then at Thorne. I gazed at Bowie, who lay peacefully on the couch. "It wasn't for anything. It was a prayer against poisoning."

Suddenly, it hit me. I sat on the floor and sobbed. "We need to have the police check if Blane was poisoned. Bob, call Stan. Have him alert Alan."

"Alan Jeffries? Holy shit."

"Yes," I said, "He might not be sworn in tomorrow as lieutenant governor. He may be taking the governor's oath of office instead."

CHAPTER 24

He who does not have the courage to speak up for his rights cannot earn the respect of others.
—Rene G. Torres

John phoned Bob and requested Thorne come along, in case he needed legal representation.

The laptop, a few blank disks, a briefcase with my notes, and I was ready to tackle the evening. I locked what I felt might be evidence in the trunk, and sat in the backseat of the truck. Bob and Thorne sat in front for more leg room.

"Why the polygraph?" Thorne asked as we pulled out of the driveway.

"Parsons' request," Bob said. "When I spoke with him, he said 'I asked for a polygraph.' That's all I know concerning the test."

Reba McIntyre provided background music. "Can you hit reject, please?" I asked. "I don't want to yell."

"Sorry." Bob said.

"Much better. I did a paper on polygraphs my senior year. Thank God. Now if I do have to write something—or answer questions—I have a base of knowledge. Can we stop at the barn? I have that paper filed in my office. I know right where it is."

"Sure thing," Bob said, "Remember, the media will try to bury Parsons. This could be a huge story."

"I know. Any tips?" I trusted Bob's media instincts. I had to. I'd fallen for him when he was a TV political news-caster.

"The less said, the better. Stick to three talking points. That's it. No matter what they say—or press *you* to say, stick to those three points. I'd suggest you use the follow-ing: that Parsons asked for the exam, that he's been a friend of Blane's for years, and that Blane came to see him to congratulate him privately before all the festivities began. Just suggestions, mind you."

"Want my new job?" A nervous giggle escaped.

"Not a chance in hell, babe."

"How about you, Thorne?" I asked.

"I think I'll have a job once we get there. Sounds to me like someone might need a lawyer."

The stop at the cabin took less than two minutes. An excellent filing system paid off. "R" for research. There was the paper—research notes attached.

I needed to think. Process. Plan.

I returned to the truck and tapped for Thorne to roll down the window.

"Can you get the portable cassette player from the glove box for me—along with Handel's *Water Music*, please?"

"Oh boy," Bob said. "Ritual time for my wife."

I love it when he says *mah wahf*.

"She plays *Moonlight Sonata* when she's melancholy, *Canon in D* when she's upset, *Water Music* when she needs to focus."

Thorne laughed. "Nothing for when she's—"

I reached through the window and thumped him on the head. "*Bolero*, of course." Men.

I stretched my legs and climbed into the truck, put the headset over my ears, and thumbed through the notes I'd taken on polygraphic examinations.

> *. . . they are based on psychophysiology. What goes on inside the person being examined. Certain things happen physiologically when we feel threatened. It is nature's way of preparing us for attack . . . calling the exam a lie detector is incorrect. It does not detect lies. It is a 100% accurate record of what is going on inside the person at the time of the question. It records human physiology . . .*

"Hey, guys, listen to this." I removed my headset and read from my paper.

"Polygraphs check relative blood pressure, the tidal volume of lungs, and moisture on skin. The blood pressure reading will show an elevated heart rate—your BP increases when in survival mode. The tidal volume checks the lungs for intake of oxygen. Your body temp goes up and you sweat . . . all of these things happen when we choose to fight."

Blane nodded his head. "And polygraphs are accepted within the general scientific community—same as DNA, fingerprints, and hair samples, did you know that? Big case—U.S. v. Frye—so Parsons better be damned sure he thinks before he speaks. John too."

"Great."

Bob didn't comment.

I continued listening to Handel and finished reading the notes, then realized we hadn't had a decent meal all day. "I know we need to get to Jackson, but could we swing through some place to eat?"

"It'll need to be a drive-thru," Bob said. "We can have something more substantial once things are settled."

"Better make those meals macho," I said.

I opened the plastic bowls filled with Bowie's food and water, blessed the food, and the four of us ate in the car. Bob and Thorne chatted about the coming year as we drove the final ten miles to the station.

"Say, hon, when did the doc say Bowie could get that cast off?"

"We have to take her in for another round of x-rays next week."

"Hey," Thorne said, "I thought we were all going to Texas after the inauguration. You have a vet there?"

"No we don't," Bob said, "but A&M turns out the best vets around. I'm sure there are tons of great doggie docs in the area."

"We're taking her to Dallas," I said.

"We're what? Did you flunk Texas geography, babe?" Bob looked at Thorne and shook his head. "We don't live near Dallas."

"Don't you want the best doctor to make sure she's healing? The best vet is in Dallas. We're taking her to Dallas." I wasn't about to compromise.

Thorne turned and looked at the pup, then at me. "I'm sure there's a good explanation, right?"

"Yeah. Explain this to us," Bob said.

"Sweeper and Striker, Ace Edwards' cats—they go to a vet in Dallas. That doctor has to be the best in Texas or Ace wouldn't go there. Enough said. It's settled."

"Who the hell is Ace Edwards?" Thorne asked.

"The best private eye in Texas," Bob said. "Great guy. I might see if he wants to come down next week. He'd keep Vic's mind off her troubles."

"Bob!" I yelled. "You are incorrigible!"

We turned into the parking lot and I began to sweat. It was 15 degrees outside and I was sweating.

"Good thing I'm not being questioned."

Bob opened my door, looked at me, and said, "You okay?"

"Just a little anxiety attack. I've been away from the political maelstrom since you left the ring."

"Think you can handle it?" Bob asked.

That was all I needed. I took a deep breath and said, "You bet. Take the pup. I've got the laptop."

We were stopped at the door. After Thorne showed his identification and explained he was Mr. Gaynor's attorney, he was escorted away by a trooper.

A second trooper approached us. "Your identification, please?" We showed him our drivers' licenses and waited.

"No dogs allowed, sir."

"I'm sorry, but—"

"But this is a registered investigative animal." I interrupted as I pointed to the cast. "Injured on the job, poor thing."

Bob bit his lip.

The trooper wasn't buying it. "Miss, I've never heard of an investigative animal."

"Michigan is so behind." I shook my head. "Have you never heard of ML, the cat? Or Hitchock? He assists Detective Ingrid Beaumont. *Okay. So I took some creative license.* You can check this particular P.I. pup's credentials with Ace Edwards in Dallas, Texas, if you'd like. He would be the one—"

"Keep the dog under control and on a leash. Any disturbance and she's caged and escorted out." I knew one day my babbling would pay off.

Bob looked at the trooper. "We would like to see Mr. Gaynor, please. I'm his son."

"He's with his attorney."

"Could you let him know we're here."

The trooper left. When he returned, he motioned for us to follow him.

"You can join them."

"Thank you."

Bob knocked. When we entered, he and his father embraced, with Bowie in between.

"How'd you get the pup in?" John asked.

"My wife. With any luck, we won't be struck by lightning."

John smiled. His face was drawn and pale, his clothes rumpled. Not the look one expects from such a powerful man.

I hugged him and said, "John, I have a few questions. I need you to be absolutely honest with me. First, did you retain Thorne?"

"Yes. He can stay. Go on. I want this over with."

"Why did you ask Stan to be your executor? Why didn't you ask your personal attorney, or even Thorne? Or your son?"

"I had my attorney as my executor. Once Blane started spouting off about Binnie I felt it would be best to have an old friend, rather than an attorney. If anything got out about the trial—or me—well, you know. Attorneys—no offense intended, Thorne—but attorneys tend to flap their mouths if the price is right. I didn't want anyone buying information. Stan is above reproach. More than I can say for some attorneys. I just needed to have someone I could trust completely."

"Sounds right to me, Beth." Bob said. "Thorne, any thoughts on that?"

"I'm sorry you think I could be bought, but you know the details of your estate. I don't. I'm sure you did what you thought you had to. I would like to know what was so secret?"

John rubbed his eyes. The fatigue showed in the lines on his face. His voice quivered. "This is attorney-client, right?"

"Right," Thorne said.

"Beth and Bob already know. I influenced the outcome of Binnie's trial. Well, to be exact, I arranged the sting."

"Okay, so we're dealing with a crime. That would be motive for murder. With Blane dead—"

"Hell! Don't you think I know how this looks? I'm telling you, I had nothing to do with this. I swear to you!"

"John, look at me," I said. "Did you and Lydia discuss the case? Did she know about Binnie?"

Thorne shot me a look.

I nodded at John. "Answer me."

"Absolutely not. I didn't discuss the case with Stan—just that I wanted a file I gave him opened and given to the authorities if something should happen to me. Why the hell would I tell Lydia, of all people?"

"Yeah," Thorne said. "What does she have to do with this?"

"It's alright. Just covering all the bases, ya know?"

Bob, a sleeping pup still in his arms, asked, "John, do you know of anyone who would want Blane harmed in any way?"

"For the love of God, I don't. If he had something on Parsons, maybe him. Parson's isn't the most upright guy. Maybe Blane wanted a judicial appointment and was blackmailing Parsons. Who the hell knows? Ask him. They're giving me a polygraph. Shit."

"It's okay," I said. "They'll only be asking about the death of Blane. Anything else wouldn't be admissible, am I right, Thorne?"

"That's right. This is what they call an investigative polygraph. The answers will be 'yes' or 'no' and all the questions will relate to this incident."

"John, Thorne will stay with you. We have some things to do."

"Sure. Before you leave, how's Binnie? Is she okay?"

"She's just fine," Bob said. "She's at the Amway with Victoria. Thanks for offering your suite. It's a great diversion for Vic and a treat for Robin."

"Okay. Just as long as she's fine. She's a good woman."

Bob and I smiled and exited the room.

"We would like to see Mr. Parsons now, please," Bob said to the trooper in the hallway. "He's expecting us."

"He's about to take a polygraph. We're waiting for the examiner to arrive."

We entered the room to find Lt. Governor Jim Parsons pale, sweating, and shaking. Shelly was with him.

"Where are the boys, Shelly?" I gave her a hug. "You need help?"

"No." Shelly blew her nose and coughed. "On top of everything, I've caught a cold. The boys are with my parents. We had so many last-minute arrangements to tend to—"

Bob asked, "Jim, have you called an attorney?"

Shelly shook her head. "No, he was about to call the state attorney general, see what he'd advise."

"Thorne's here, if you need him."

"Lydia's Thorne?" The governor-elect laughed. "I knew she'd try and ingratiate me somehow."

I didn't have the heart to tell him she hates him.

Looking at Bob, Parsons spat, "Keep that damn dog away from me."

I thought back to when Bowie bit Parsons. "Sir, do you remember—did you have anything in your pockets when Bowie jumped and . . ." I gave a *you know* nod toward his crotch. It was humiliating enough that the dog bit him there. I didn't want to verbalize it.

"Sure do. I'd just been chatting with Lydia. She's been hounding me for a job. She had a fresh can of mixed nuts. I put some in my pockets—for a snack—you know?"

"That's why she attacked you, sir! It wasn't *you* she was after, it was your nuts!" The minute the words left my mouth, I turned a shade Robin might call raunchy red.

Bob sighed, Shelly gasped, and Parsons said, "Holy shit. I want you to speak for me? I *am* desperate."

"Oh no . . . what I meant was . . . you know—"

"That's quite alright, Mrs. Larken, we know." Parsons wiped his forehead with his shirtsleeve.

"Did you discuss anything else with Lydia, or just a job?" Bob asked.

"No, wasn't at her desk long. Her voice irritates me. Took the nuts, then she asked if all the positions were filled in my administration and suggested I use a smoker's patch."

"She *what?*" My heart started to race. "She didn't know you were already on the patch?"

"Apparently not. She'd gotten me a box of patches as an inauguration gift. I didn't want to appear rude, so I thanked her. Told her I'd been using them for awhile but appreciated it. Which I did. She handed me the box. They were stronger than the ones I'd been using, so I took one out of the box, removed the patch I had on, and replaced it."

"And you tossed the old patch in her trash, am I correct?" I asked.

"I sure did. Right in front of her. To show my appreciation and all." He beamed. "She offered me the whole box. In fact, I gave one to Blane when he came by—to help him out."

The examiner came to the door and motioned for Parsons. "Right this way, please."

Shelly gave her husband a kiss on the cheek, and fussed with the little hair he had.

"We'll be back in a bit," I said.

Bob smiled at Shelly. "You take care. If you need anything, let us know."

"Thank you, thank you both."

Bob and I took Bowie to the car where we could talk in private.

"Turn the heater up—it's cold!" I said.

"So, what do you think?" Bob asked.

"I think I need to give the investigators the items I collected."

Chapter 25

The ultimate measure of a man is not where
he stands in moments of comfort, but where
he stands at times of challenge and controversy.
—*Martin Luther King, Jr.*

"Beth, you can't believe Lydia was involved," Bob said.

"I don't want to think that, but everything points to her. You heard what Parsons said. He wouldn't lie, Bob. Not facing an inauguration and a polygraph. And why would he lie about Lydia and the patch?"

Bob slumped and looked at the floorboard. "He wouldn't. Okay. Let's get this over with."

"Oh no, Bob, look." I pointed at the vans entering the parking lot.

"Aw shit. The media. How the hell did they find out?"

"Take Bowie. Huddle down to protect her from the wind. I'll handle them. It's my job. Now go." What an initiation.

The cameramen were getting their gear together—setting up floodlights and adjusting lenses. When we left the truck, one male affiliate reporter barged from the station's van and headed our way. Bob continued through the door. I stopped short.

"Excuse me," the man said. He wore a hooded parka and shoved a cordless microphone in my face.

"Yes?" I did my *look him in the eye* routine. He didn't hold my stare, but looked at the ground.

"May I pass, please? I'm with CNN."

"That's nice. I see your pass. I'm not wearing mine at the moment."

"Oh, what affiliate do you represent?"

"I'm out of Lansing." This cat and mouse game amused me.

"Really? Radio, television, or print?"

"All of the above. I'm with the press corps for the new state administration. I'm Beth Larken." We exchanged a hearty handshake.

"We understand Lieutenant Governor Parsons is being questioned in the death of former Judge Blane MacGowan. Is that correct?"

Think of the talking points. "The governor-elect has been a friend of Judge MacGowan for years."

"Is it true Parsons saw MacGowan prior to his death?"

"Judge MacGowan went to see Governor-Elect Parsons to congratulate him privately before the inauguration. For the record, it was not immediately prior to his death."

"When was it, then?" the reporter pressed.

"Please excuse me. There are no further comments at this time." I walked into the building, took a deep breath, and congratulated myself. *I did it and I did it on my own.*

I approached the officer behind the front desk. "If any of the media want statements, they are to speak with me. No one but me. Please tell them I will make a formal statement in one-half hour. Is there a conference room we can use?"

"Yes, ma'am. I'll make sure it's available for your use."

Down the hall I found Bob and Bowie with Shelly. "You look exhausted," I said to her.

"I am. I called the boys. Told them what was going on. Well, not exactly. I told them Jim was answering some questions about Blane since they'd been together earlier."

"Shelly, did you use a hard line?" I looked at Bob, who closed his eyes and groaned.

"No, I used my cell phone."

"That answers that," I said.

Bob sat next to Shelly, the pup still cradled in his arms. "You know better, Shelly. The media is now crawling all over this place."

Shelly began to cry. "I'm not thinking straight. Jim will be furious."

"No he won't," I assured her. "I handled it. I'm making a formal statement in a while. We need to wait until after the polygraph."

I'd barely finished my sentence when Parsons walked in, smiling. Shelly hugged him and told him the media had arrived.

"I've begun my job, sir," I said, trying to keep the mood light. "We'll discuss salary later. I warn you, though, it'll be hefty."

"We'll see how the budget looks. Thank you."

The examiner joined us.

"What were your findings?" I asked.

"Four readings were taken. That's standard." He showed me the printout.

"The top reading checks chest breathing, the second, stomach breathing. The green line represents the moisture surface of the skin, and the red line is the cardio reading. In my opinion, based on my education, experience, and training, Lieutenant Governor James W. Parsons does not believe he has any involvement in the death of former Judge Blane MacGowan."

Parsons grabbed the examiner's hand. "Thank you, thank you very much."

Shelly went into the hallway and called for a trooper. "Can we leave now? My husband has an inaugural speech to prepare."

"Yes, he's free to leave. We might need to question you further, sir, but it will be in a few days, once we have the autopsy results."

I turned to Parsons. "Will you want me to give a prepared statement, sir, or would you like to speak with the press?"

"It's time we get used to being on the same team. How about we do it together?"

Bob walked over and whispered, "I need to talk with you. *Now.* In private."

"Excuse us, please," I said.

We shut the door after we left. Bob still whispered. "You really *are* taking that job? We didn't talk about it—

you just took it. We have a trip to Texas tomorrow night—right after the inauguration. You can't leave Lansing so soon—if you're working for the governor."

Bowie must have felt the tension. She opened her eyes, squirmed, and looked around. "Shhhhhhhh. *Todo el correcto, muchacha.* It's okay, girl."

"If the Administration needs me badly enough, they'll let me call the shots. If I'm going to work, it's going to be on *my* terms. I'm working on positive PR and that's it. Today was job insurance." My turn to wink.

"I love you, Mrs. Larken."

"I love you, too, Bob Larken. Now let's go see your dad before I conduct that press conference."

We found Thorne and John in a waiting room down the hall.

"Everyone holding up in here?" Bob asked.

Thorne shrugged. "John took the polygraph. It came back 'inconclusive.'"

"What does that mean?" Bob asked Thorne.

"It means that, based on the findings, they can neither confirm nor deny John's involvement in Blane's death."

John grumbled, "And that son of a bitch kept saying 'don't play games with me.' Hell, I wasn't playing games. This is my *life*, why would I play games? He treated me like a damn criminal."

"John, calm down," I said. "He doesn't know you from Adam. For all he knows you *are* a criminal."

"Inconclusive, shit. What does *that* mean?" John asked. "I don't know anything about Blane's death. I swear to you!"

"I don't think I should be here for this—I'm working for Parsons now. I'm sorry. I have a press conference to attend." I gave all three men hugs and kissed the top of Bowie's head.

"Break a leg, sweetie," Bob said.

I looked at Bowie's cast. "Great. We'd be twins. I'll let you know when we're finished."

As I strolled down the hallway, I strategized. *Remember the three talking points.*

I stopped and freshened up in the ladies room, then bought a bottled water and a package of M&Ms from the machine. Nothing like chocolate to calm my nerves.

It only took two gulps to down the candy. I wonder what the world's record is for chocolate consumption? Something to research.

I approached the trooper at the front desk. "Can you tell me what room is being used for the press conference, please?"

He pointed and said, "First door on the left."

"Thank you."

I looked through the wall of windows and didn't see any media types wandering around. Of course, it was dark, but I assumed everyone was set up and ready to hear the official statement.

"Excuse me, sir," I said to the same trooper, "is there a media liaison officer who can make a statement?"

"He will be there in about five minutes. The name is Officer Bradley. He's getting some information from Forensics."

"Okay. Thanks again."

I waited outside the designated room. I needed to enter with Parsons and the officer. I didn't want to go in before them and be bombarded. *I can do this.*

Parsons rounded the corner. "You ready for the cameras, Mrs. Larken? Anything I should know?"

"I'm ready. Leave it to me. All you should say is, I'm saddened by the death of a longtime friend. It's a tragic accident. I have an inauguration to prepare for, thank you."

"I shouldn't mention my innocence?" he asked.

"No! Do not give them any indication that you were even considered a suspect. An officer will be discussing Forensics. I'd like to speak with him first. When I do, please, sir, remain silent."

Parsons looked over my shoulder and said, "Looks like the show is about to begin."

I turned and greeted the officer. "You must be Officer Bradley. I'm Beth Larken with Lieutenant Governor Parson's office. Do you know the lieutenant governor?" The men shook hands and exchanged pleasantries.

"Before we go inside, I'd like to ask a few questions. What were the findings?"

"It appears that Mr. MacGowan's accident was deliberate."

"Wait—I need to see the officer in charge of this case. Stay with the lieutenant governor. Do *not* let anyone near him!" Something clicked in my brain. I didn't want to leave anything to chance.

I found Officer Karlisa, the officer handling the questioning. I explained my suspicions and requested the Olds Building be shut off from communications.

"I am in authority to speak for the current administration. We need to have the phone system disconnected until after midnight. We need to make sure no one remains in that building except for the front guard and Lydia— Governor Melvin's assistant. Call M-Fone, her cell phone provider—have them temporarily disconnect her number."

Maybe I wasn't *officially* speaking for the administration, but I'd worry later about any ramifications if my instincts were off. I didn't think they were.

"Officer Bradley, sir," I said. "I'm ready. Anything else I should know before we begin?"

The officer had no further comments and didn't allow time for more questions. He opened the doors. Lights and a barrage of questions greeted us.

"Can you tell us why the lieutenant governor was questioned?"

"Why did Judge MacGowan meet with the lieutenant governor?"

"Had the Judge been drinking?"

I took the informal stage. A few moments later I was joined by Parsons and Officer Bradley. "As you know, Lieutenant Governor Parsons was a long-time friend of Judge Blane MacGowan." More questions were shouted. One man, in front, asked for my name.

"My name is Beth Larken, L-A-R-K-E-N. I am the press liaison for the new administration. I ask you to please, please hold your questions. Again, the lieutenant governor and Mr. MacGowan had been friends for years. Mr. MacGowan came to the lieutenant governor's office to offer his congratulations before leaving on a brief vacation."

A woman in the rear interrupted. "Can you tell us why the Judge would leave on vacation and miss the inauguration?"

"I'm sorry. That would be speculation."

Jim Parsons and Officer Bradley remained silent.

I continued. "We have learned that Mr. MacGowan did make several phone calls some time prior to his death, but they were cut short. As you know, the reception in the Irish Hills is poor for cell phone usage. Officer Bradley of the Michigan State Police is here with more details. Officer Bradley?"

"Thank you, Ms. Larken. We have run preliminary toxicology tests. It appears that Mr. MacGowan was poisoned. A rash was apparent on his right forearm, consistent with irritation present in skin contact with various poisons. Blood levels indicate that the poison was cyanide."

"What did the rash have to do with the poisoning?" a reporter shouted.

"It was consistent with rashes found—"

More questions cut his response short.

"I'm sorry," I said. "Our time is up. Lieutenant Governor, do you have anything to say?"

A weary-looking Jim Parsons stepped to the microphone, wiped his eyes, and said, "I'm saddened by the death of a longtime friend. It's a tragic occurrence. I have an inauguration to prepare for, thank you."

"That's all for now," I said. "Thank you."

The three of us left the room. I thanked Officer Bradley and pushed Parsons down the hall. "Move it. Now!"

I shoved him through a doorway. When I saw the room was empty I whispered, "I know exactly what happened to Blane. Bowie found the clues."

"The dog? What the hell are you talking about?"

"You were supposed to die. You were the target!"

Chapter 26

Nearly all men can stand adversity, but if you want to test a man's character, give him power.
—*Abraham Lincoln*

"Oh God, me?" Parsons leaned against the tiled wall. Sweat broke out on his forehead and he licked his moustache. "I need something to drink. Is there a water fountain nearby? Oh my God."

"Let's get you back to your wife. I'll get you some water." I held on to a shaking Jim Parsons. "The two of you need to get home."

"What the hell—your dog figured this out? Don't shit me, I have a right to know what's going on."

"You will, just let me take what we've discovered to the authorities first. Please, sir, have a trooper drive you home. We'll see you at the inauguration. Everything will be over soon. I promise."

"Shit," he said, wiping the sweat off his brow. "I'm trusting a Larken. "

I located Officer Bradley and explained my theory. He listened, nodded a lot, and took notes. Exhausted and hungry by now, I wanted to go home, but knew we couldn't. Not yet.

I spotted Bob exiting the men's room. "Honey, where's Bowie?"

"With Thorne and John. Everything go alright with Parsons and the media sharks?"

"Yes. Let me tell you, they're ruthless! How did you do that all those years?"

"Adrenaline. Sheer adrenaline."

He put his arm around me and escorted me down the hall. "Thorne's advising John—but I think everything will be okay. With Blane gone, who will prosecute? Robin? Not sure that would happen, but you never know. To our knowledge no one knows about the money exchange except for you, Vic, Thorne, and me. Blane might have told Parsons that Robin was framed, but it doesn't appear as though he mentioned John. If Blane had implicated John, you *know* Parsons would have sung like the proverbial canary."

"Or, in this case," I said, "a robin."

Bob smiled. "True, and he would love to see me and my dad fry. Thorne said the District Attorney could step in, but how would they find out?"

"You don't suppose Robin told anyone, do you?"

Bob looked down the empty hallway and said, "I don't think she knows money was involved. From what John told me, she only knows she was put there for her own protection, but only time will tell."

I sighed. "More silence required."

Bob kissed me on top of my head and said, "To that I have no comment."

"Well, I have a theory on Blane's death. I went to the officer in charge with it. Did you know Blane was poisoned?"

"Holy shit." He stopped, looked at me, and grabbed my shoulders. His voice raised, his eyes widened. "What the hell happened?"

I explained what Forensics had discovered, my ideas, what I'd done to ensure Lydia's ignorance of the news, and my plan.

"Let's do it then, babe," he said.

Bob opened the door and we entered the small room where John and Thorne sat. "Hi guys! There's our wounded warrior!" I took Bowie from Thorne's arms and said, "Well, can you two leave?"

"Yes, but I can't leave the state until this is settled," John said. "This is absurd. I was supposed to go to Texas with you. The plane's all chartered. A ten-seater. I wasn't sure who'd be going. Now *I'm* the one that can't go."

"Let's see," Bob said. "We have Lydia and Thorne, Binnie, Beth's dad, the three of us—we were going to have Vic and Blane. And you, of course. That would have been ten. Thorne probably shouldn't go, in case you need him."

"No, no, no," John protested. "Thorne should go. If I need him, he can be back here in a matter of hours. Not a problem."

"Well," I said, "first things first. We need to head to the capitol. Lydia, Bitsy, and Stan will be expecting us at midnight. Does Lydia know where you are, Thorne?"

"No. You said to keep this confidential. She assumes I'm at your place with everyone else."

"Okay," I said. "I thought ahead and set the house phone to forward calls to my cell. She hasn't called."

"Why the secrecy? She probably knows now. It's been all over the radio. She would have heard you with Parsons."

"Nope," I said. "Her radio isn't on her desk. When all this happened, Stan moved it into the conference room. That door is locked. She's in the dark, news-wise. There's no one but her at the Olds Building. Everyone left at noon—New Year's Eve." I couldn't look at Bob.

"She likes it that way, to be honest," Thorne said. "She wanted these last few hours alone, at her desk. I think she's getting melancholy."

Right on cue Bob said, "I called Stan. He said Bitsy was too tired to hang around. They went home to take a little nap. Frankly, I don't think they want to usher in the New Year with any type of celebration."

"I can understand that," I said. "Not exactly the way we intended things to go."

I hung my head and avoided Bob's eyes. I needed to stall. Let the investigators have enough time to follow through with my ideas. "Let's grab dinner first, then get to Lansing."

"Great idea, babe."

Bob tossed Thorne the keys. "Why don't you bring the truck around back? I can't wait to see a city slickin' attorney drive an extended cab diesel. Wish I had a camera for this. Plus, if there's any media lurking, they won't follow *you*—they'll be looking for one of us. My wife's a celebrity now."

After an endless meal at an off-the-beaten-path diner I knew, we arrived at the state's capital city at eleven-thirty. Still too early. "How about stopping for coffee?" I asked.

Bob played along. "I could use a cup before breaking open the bubbly at midnight. Oh shoot! The champagne! We need to get some. Beth, know of a place near here?"

"Sure do." I turned to Thorne and John. "You guys, get a seat at the all-night diner by the offices and Bob and I will go to the liquor store. Order us each coffee, okay?"

"Hey, Uncle Thorne?" Bob asked. "Mind carrying the diva dog with you? And while you're at it—here." Bob took a hot water bottle out from under his seat and tossed it to Thorne. "Could you have them warm this up at the diner?"

"What the hell? A hot water bottle?" Thorne scooped Bowie, still wrapped in her pink blanket, into his arms.

Bob looked at Thorne and smiled. "Yeah. Have them warm it for her. It's frigid out here. Don't want her to get a chill when we walk to the Olds."

"You kids are nuts," John said. "And speaking of the Olds Building, why can't we go grab Lydia early? She can join us," John said.

"Nope," I said. "A promise is a promise. We told her midnight."

"Alright, then," Thorne said. "Get plenty of champagne. Tonight might be the perfect night to drown our sorrows."

Bob looked up to the stars. "And here we thought it was going to be a celebration."

We parked at the Olds Building. John and Thorne walked to the diner with Bowie, and Bob and I headed for the liquor store. I took my cell phone out of my pocket and showed it to Bob.

"I set it on *vibrate* so no one could hear it if it rang."

After buying four bottles of Dom Perignon, we headed to the diner.

"All set to pop the cork!" Bob announced as we joined John and Thorne.

"Excuse me, fellas, the ladies room is calling me." I left the table and headed to the back of the diner as the phone rattled in my pocket. It was the state troopers calling.

"Hello, This is Beth Larken . . . yes . . . I understand. We'll be there. Thank you." I looked at my watch and took a deep breath.

I returned to the table and sat next to Bob. "Ahhhhh, much better." I placed my hand on his thigh and patted him to let him know the call had been received.

"The year is winding down," Bob said. "It's been bittersweet, hasn't it?"

"Sure has." John grimaced. "Margaret's death, you two meeting . . . your beautiful wedding—"

"I found out you're my dad and now, there's Robin." Bob's eyes misted over. "A year filled with emotion, that's for sure."

"And," Thorne said, "Lydia and I are engaged. Doesn't get any better." He glanced at the clock on the wall. "Speaking of my sweetie—let's get a move on."

I took a deep breath. Much as I wanted to get this over with, I dreaded the aftermath. "Okay! Let's get back to the Olds and ring in the New Year!"

Chapter 27

Some people like to understand what they believe in,
while others like to believe in what they understand.
—*Stanislaw J. Lec*

Police cars surrounded the building. Uniformed officers, guns drawn, yelled, "Stay back, folks!" when they
saw us.

"What the hell?" Thorne rushed towards the police.

"I said *stand back!*"

"You don't understand. My fiancée is inside. Oh my
God, what's wrong?"

Thorne looked at us—panic crossed his face. "My God,
is she alright? Please, what's going on?"

I looked at Bob. He grabbed his father and said, "Stay
here. Just stay here and keep your mouth shut." John
pulled his jacket collar up and shoved his hands in his
pockets.

Bob handed the pup to me and approached his best
friend. "Thorne, please," he said. "Please stand back."

Thorne looked at Bob, then over to me. "What the hell . . ."

Lydia appeared in the doorway, surrounded by state troopers, handcuffed and crying.

"Lydia!" Thorne screamed. "Don't say a word! Not a word!"

He ran through the barricades and yelled, "I'm her attorney. My name is David Hawthorne."

Lydia sobbed. "I didn't mean it. I'm so sorry. The patch was for Parsons. I swear."

"Not another word, Lydia!" Thorne screamed. "She's under duress. Let me talk with her. I'm her attorney!"

Lydia collapsed.

An officer walked up to Thorne and said, "You can meet us at the station, sir."

"Why do you have her handcuffed? Please, get her a doctor."

"She's being taken in for questioning concerning the death of former Judge Blane MacGowan and the attempted murder of Lieutenant Governor James W. Parsons."

Thorne called to us, "This is absurd! Go on—I'm going with Lydia. Someone please get her medical help."

"Dear Scholar and Martyr," I prayed to Saint Thomas More. ". . . Perfect in your honesty and love of truth, grant that lawyers and judges may imitate you and achieve true justice for all people. Amen."

We watched as Thorne got into a patrol car and left.

"Let's go home. There's nothing more we can do," I said. "Thorne will be busy. You can call him later. We all need some rest."

The three of us, plus a snoring B.A.D. got in the truck, turned up the heat, and headed home.

Suddenly Bob slammed his fist on the steering wheel, interrupting our private, separate trains of thought. "I feel like I let my best friend down. We should have let him know ahead of time."

"Bob, honey, we don't know what he might have done. He loves Lydia. If we tipped him off—"

"Yeah," John said. "A desperate man—you never know. Trust me. I've done some pretty damn stupid shit for love."

The short drive home was completed in silence.

"John, help yourself to the couch. I'm gonna take a shower. See if I can't wash some of the day's crap off."

Bob headed upstairs. I put Bowie's plastic bootie over her cast for a short walk. As she sniffed the ground, I looked at the frozen Looking Glass River, then up to the heavens. "Mama, did I do the right thing?" Tears flowed as I realized the enormity of the past few days' events.

Bowie limped as far as her leash would allow, sniffed, squatted, and returned to where I stood with a stick in her mouth. I picked her up, gave her hug, and tossed the branch back on the ground. "Time to go in, girl. We have a long day ahead of us tomorrow."

Bob joined us in bed, petted Bowie, and said, "Looks like we have a little hero, hey? *Manera de ir, muchacha.* Way to go, girl." He stared up at the ceiling with his arm resting on the pup.

"Honey, there's nothing we can do for Thorne right now. He needs to do his job, and his job is helping Lydia."

"I knew she hated Parsons, but I had no idea—"

"None of us did, sweetheart." I leaned over and kissed his cheek. "I didn't believe her when she said she'd rather see him dead than be our next governor. How were we to know?"

"God." He closed his eyes. "Poor Thorne. I can't imagine."

"Let's get some sleep, honey. Tomorrow is a big day."

Bob began snoring before I could say, "I love you." I placed Bowie in her bed, pink-casted leg sticking over the edge, but I wasn't quite ready for sleep. My brain meandered to Shelly and her husband. They were about to become Michigan's first couple. I hadn't decided whether I was envious or relieved to be out of the limelight. With my new job, maybe I had the best of both worlds. Shelly and Jim had been through hell and back. I'm not really sure that's a life I'd want now. I like the idea of settling in Texas and raising a family. Having our place here in Grand Ledge. Blending both our homes into one. I rolled over, whispered "I love you" to my husband, and thanked God for the arrival of a new year. Maybe we could finally break out from the silence.

The phone rang. I looked at the clock. Eight o'clock in the morning. "Hello?" I grumbled.

"Get your ass downstairs, girl! We're on the porch."

Vic. I should have known.

"What? You're where?"

"On your porch. We were gonna ring the doorbell except we heard snoring. Sounds like a chain saw in there."

"Oh. That's John. Gimme a minute. He's on the couch. We don't have the spare bedroom fixed up yet."

"It's cold, Chrissy. Move it!"

I was the one to hang up this time.

"Bob. Bob! Get up. Vic and Robin are here and John's still asleep on the couch."

He opened his eyes and said, "Huh?"

"Robin—Vic. They're here. We need to get a move on."

"Oh God. John's here. Now Robin's here?"

He crawled from under the comforter and went to the bathroom. I threw my robe on, ran my fingers through my hair, and joined him. "Pass me the toothpaste."

I put a dab in my mouth and headed downstairs. Fresh as a dead daisy.

I poked John. "We've got company. Move it."

He groaned and rolled over. I poked him again. "Robin's here."

His eyes flew open. "Shit."

"Go freshen up."

"Yeah, then I need to get home to change before the inauguration."

He left the room and I answered the door. "Happy New Year, you two!" I hugged them both as they stomped off the snow that had accumulated on their shoes.

"Robin!" I said after the two hung their coats in the entryway. Bob's mother wore a long black wool skirt and matching tunic that came well below her hips. A patterned scarf draped over one shoulder, camouflaging her ample chest, and her hair hung in soft, subdued auburn waves. Refined and elegant.

I looked at Vic, who beamed and said "Not bad, huh? We had so much fun. We have some more clothes in the car and an entire case of new cosmetics!"

"Yeah," Robin said. "Vic here taught me less is best. Don't wanna cover up m'natural beauty. That would be a sin, ain't that right, Vic?"

"Okay, fine," Vic said. "We still need some grammar lessons but, honey, you look gorgeous!" The women embraced.

Vic sat next to me and grabbed my hand. "Kiddo, you did great last night. We watched the broadcast while Robin's hair color was processing. What a shock." Tears streamed down her face.

"Now don't start," I said. "You'll get me going and your makeup—you'll ruin all that hard work."

Robin grabbed a tissue from her purse and handed it to Vic. "It's alright, honey. You've earned the right to cry, child. We can redo the makeup. You know, I never really heard much about that man of yours. Tell me about him— all the wonderful stuff. It helps to share. Believe me, honey, I know." Robin squeezed next to Vic on the couch—the three of us huddled together and listened.

"He was a good man, really he was. I know he was haunted by what he'd done because he had nightmares now and again. Just that last one—that was the only time he mentioned names. Most of the times he'd just moan and thrash around."

"Now yer talking, girl. Moanin' 'n thrashin'." Robin let loose with a laugh that would stir any ghosts that might be haunting us.

"Oh yeah." Vic smiled. "He definitely was a moaner. Why do you think he was called the Hot Scot? But he loved me, I know he did."

"I'm sure he did, sugah." Robin pushed aside a stray hair that had fallen across Vic's forehead.

"Oh, I talked to his brother. He's worried about Blane's dog. I'd forgotten about his dog. His brother can't have it. His kids are allergic. You two want another dog?" She looked at me with begging eyes.

"What kind is it?" She knows I'm a sucker for dogs.

"It's really a great dog. Kinda big, though. It's a golden and lab mix. Oh my God." She started to cry again.

"Vic, really, we'll find a home for the dog," I promised.

"It's not that—it's the dog's name. His name is Scandal."

"Oh dear me," Robin said. "Helluva name, considerin'— damn."

"The dog was at his place, then his brother took it to the vet to board him until we could figure something out."

Vic took a deep breath. "He needs a big yard. Think you could take him, Chrissy?"

"We'll see. Let's get through today. Then we have the trip to Texas. We really need a break. The Hill Country air will do you good."

"Sure will, honey." Robin's face beamed. "You're just gonna love Texas. We'll have ourselves one helluva good time."

"Blane was supposed to go. You know, it sounds stupid, but I know he'll be there with us. I just know it." Vic wasn't the most religious person, but she has her moments.

"Yes, he will be," I smiled. "And Daddy, John, Bob, and Thorne—they'll be with us, too."

"Oh God," Vic started to cry again. "Thorne. He must be devastated."

"Them two just announced their engagement. Damn, that's gotta be rough." Robin shook her newly colored red hair. "That Lydia. Damn."

"Lydia?" Vic cried. "Lydia! She's our *friend*."

I wanted to say, "And thanks to our *friend* your honey died alone and poisoned in the Irish Hills, never knowing what was happening to him," but thought better of it. Best to just get through this day and then sort it all out. I muttered a quick prayer to Saint Benedict. He handles poisonings.

Robin shrugged. "I guess she had one of them breakdowns. Nutted up. Lost it. One of them passion things ya read 'bout. Nasty stuff. Plum miserable."

"Thorne's with her," Bob said as he entered the room. "Good morning, ladies." He kissed Vic, wiped her tears with his thumb, and did a double-take when he saw Robin.

"See?" Robin placed her hands on her hips and spun around like an agile teen. "Told ya this is where yer good looks come from."

John entered the room. "I take exception to that comment."

Robin walked up to him and said, "Well, looky here. You don't look a day over seventy-five, you ole coot!"

He smiled. "Charming as ever, dear." He kissed her briefly on one cheek, then the other.

"He always tried to impress me with them fancy manners," she said.

"Good to see you, Robin. You're as beautiful as ever."

"Oh damn." Victoria sobbed. "Love. I can't take it."

"Honey child, it's okay." Robin put her arm around Vic. "They know'd who done it now. Justice. She'll get hers. The devil will see to it, ain't that right, Beth? We know about that devil business."

"We also know it's not our place to judge," I said. "Now, I need to get ready. We have an inauguration to attend."

Chapter 28

The world is round and the place which may seem like
the end may also be only the beginning.
—*Ivy Baker Priest*

Thorne waited at the side steps of the capitol building,
alone.

"I'm so sorry." I hugged him with one arm, the other
arm held Bowie. I saw he hadn't changed clothes. "You
didn't make it home."

"Kinda busy here." He nodded a greeting to John and
Robin and embraced Victoria. "I don't know what to say."

"Neither do I. Let's keep it that way," she said.

Bob stared at his best friend. Thorne was the first to
speak. "You did what you needed to do."

Bob took his hand, shook it, but didn't make eye contact. "Let's get seated."

The day was picture perfect, weather-wise. January 1.
This year promised to be a record breaker. The sun was out,
not a cloud in the sky, although the temperature was chilly.
We all dressed warmly, since the swearing-in ceremonies

would be held on the steps of the Capitol. Then Governor Parsons, Lieutenant Governor Jeffries, Secretary of State Shriner, and Attorney General Olexa would lead a motor processional a few blocks to where speeches would be given, inside the Lansing Center, the city's largest convention center. Parsons chose to give his speech at the Capitol.

Our seats were directly behind the families of the new governor and his wife. The children of Lieutenant Governor Jeffries sat to our left. Shelly Parsons sat on the stage, holding the Bible that would be used for the oath of office. Next to her sat outgoing Governor Melvin and his wife, Bitsy. Local high school bands played patriotic music as the crowd gathered.

John was shaking. From the cold or from nerves, I couldn't tell. He looked at me, then at Bob. His eyes glazed over with tears as he said over the background noise, "I'm retiring. I've had enough. This ordeal made me realize that my family means more to me than money or power. You can't put a price tag on this kind of love. Because of me, deliberately or not, I've caused so much pain. I am going to do something worthwhile with what remains of my life. I don't want to be haunted by the silence of the past."

Bob and I inhaled the winter's air as we processed what John had said.

"I think our trip will help with the healing," Bob said. "Nothing cures what ails a person's soul like the Hill Country. I love Michigan, but Texas really is home."

Bob kissed me and said, "Excuse me," and headed for

the makeshift stage where everyone had been seated. He smiled and waved as the cameras rolled.

"Ladies and gentlemen, may I have your attention, please? It is my honor and privilege to have the State of Michigan High School Honor Band accompany me in the singing of our National Anthem. Please rise."

I looked at John and Robin as they put their hands over their hearts and sang along with their son. I looked at Victoria and Thorne, who had both suffered great losses yesterday. And I looked at my husband, a proud man who seemed to have made his peace, for now, with being on the sidelines. His voice rose with passion and clarity as he sang. This was the day he'd dreamt of—inauguration day. After the drama and tension of the last few days, sitting here with my circle of loved ones seemed like something out of a dream.

> *Oh say does that star-bangled banner yet wave*
> *O'er the land of the free and the home of the brave.*

As Bob's rich voice handled the dramatic final lines with ease, I thought about the irony of it all. Blane dead, Robin free, Parsons our new head of state, and Lydia, presumably, about to lose her freedom for what she had done. I looked down at Bowie in my arms, her pink cast peaking out from its matching sweater. My husband exited the stage to thunderous applause. Vic and Thorne, eyes dry, toughed it out as they gazed up at him. The home of the brave, indeed.

273

As Bob came back up the aisle to us, I saw Daddy next to him. "Sorry, I'm a bit late," he said. "Traffic was horrible."

"We saved you a seat. Nice vest," I whispered. The latest Frank Pullen creation was navy wool—embroidered with a repeated pattern of Michigan flags and state crests.

"I had it made when I thought—well, you know."

I gave him a kiss. "I love you, Daddy."

After the national anthem and invocation, it was time for the oath of office. Shelly looked down at her family, then at us. She mouthed the words *thank you*. Parsons placed his right hand on the Bible, raised his left hand, and recited the oath of office.

"I, James W. Parsons, do solemnly swear that I will support the Constitution of the United States and the constitution of this state and I will faithfully discharge the duties as Governor to the best of my ability. So help me God."

Bob and I sighed in relief as the crowd cheered and clapped.

It was time for the new governor to give his inaugural address. Bob sat next to me with clenched jaws—head erect and eyes closed.

"Ladies and gentlemen," Governor Parsons began. "Fellow citizens of Michigan, we are gathered here to celebrate a new beginning . . .I ask you to join with me in the spirit of renewal . . . No task is too great or too small . . .

We must join together to help create a better, stronger, and safer state . . . and to this end, I would like to honor an exemplary citizen, who by her observance, tenacity, and fighting spirit helped in the apprehension yesterday of a suspect in a possible murder case. May I please ask Mrs. Beth Larken to join me?"

Shocked, I handed Bowie to Bob and stood up.

"No, bring the pup," the new governor said.

Bowie snuggled next to me and nestled in my arms. The cameras and cheers didn't faze her. She held up her head and looked over the crowd.

As I joined the governor on stage, he continued. "Mrs. Larken, my wife and I, and the entire State of Michigan thank you for your assistance. Alert citizens help every day on our streets—reporting suspicious behavior and working to make this State a better place to live. We commend you. As Martin Luther King, Jr. said, 'Our lives begin to end the day we become silent about things that matter.'" The new governor passed me a note that read *Thank you for speaking up for those who have been betrayed by their own silence. Jim and Shelly.* I smiled at both the governor and his wife as he continued. "At this time, I would like Officers Bradley and Karlisa of the Michigan State Police to join us."

The officers stood on either side of me, each holding a piece of paper.

"The People of the State of Michigan," Officer Bradley said, "would like to commend Beth Larken for service above and beyond the duty of normal citizenry."

"And," Officer Karlisa said, "the People of the State of Michigan hereby designate Bowie Aloysia Dog an official K-9 Crime Chaser for sniffing out the clues necessary to put the pieces of the evidentiary puzzle together."

The audience stood, applauded, and whistled.

I accepted the certificates and kissed the top of Bowie's head. "Thank you so much Officers, Governor."

Bowie, as if on command, raised her head and howled.

Assuredly there is but one way in which to achieve what

is not merely difficult but utterly against human nature:

to love those who hate us, to repay their evil deeds with benefits,

to return blessings for reproaches. It is that we remember

not to consider men's evil intention but to look upon

the image of God in them, which cancels and effaces their transgressions,

and with its beauty and dignity allures us to love and embrace them.

—*John Calvin*

Beth's Bibliography
of Patron Saints

Benedict – poisonings

Blasé – cure for injuries

Clare of Assisi – good weather

Denis – strife

Dymphnau – family harmony

Francis of Assissi – animals

James – veterinarians

John – against poisoning

Joseph – married couples

Jude – lost causes

Norbert – peace

Raphael – lovers and nightmares (modern day, also travelers)

Raphael the Archangel – happy meetings

Roch – dogs

Thomas More – judges and politicians

Valentine – greeting card industry

Vincent de Paul – prisoners